Jackie Ashend[illegible] ith alpha heroes wh[illegible] ng only to have it b[illegible] heroines. She liv[illegible] with her husband, the inimitable Dr Jax, two kids and two rats. When she's not torturing alpha males and their gutsy heroines she can be found drinking chocolate martinis, reading anything she can lay her hands on, wasting time on social media, or being forced to go mountain biking with her husband. To keep up to date with Jackie's new releases and other news sign up to her newsletter at jackieashenden.com.

If you liked *King's Price* why not try

Unleashed by Caitlin Crews
Play Thing by Nicola Marsh
Look at Me by Cara Lockwood

Also by Jackie Ashenden

The Knights of Ruin

Ruined
Destroyed

Discover more at millsandboon.co.uk.

KING'S PRICE

JACKIE ASHENDEN

MILLS & BOON

First Published in Great Britain 2018
by Mills & Boon, an imprint of HarperCollins*Publishers*
1 London Bridge Street, London, SE1 9GF

ISBN: 978-0-263-93238-6

This book is produced from independently certified FSC™ paper
to ensure responsible forest management.
For more information visit www.harpercollins.co.uk/green.

Printed and bound in Spain
by CPI, Barcelona

CHAPTER ONE

Leon

'It's very simple.' I kept my back to the office as I gazed out of the floor-to-ceiling windows that gave magnificent views of Sydney's impressive harbour. 'I want your daughter.'

There was silence behind me.

Clearly, I'd shocked Thomas Hamilton—one of Sydney's most beloved and lauded philanthropists—into silence.

Excellent. Keeping him off-balance until he'd agreed to my demands was half the battle.

'What do you mean you want my daughter?' he asked.

There was a hint of unsteadiness in his voice. It was very, very slight but I heard it, oh, yes, I did.

I said nothing, letting him stew, watching the yachts in the harbour and the ferry sailing towards Manly, the sunlight touching on the white curves of the iconic Opera House.

Christ, I loved Sydney. Bright and flashy and sexy, with a dark, dirty underbelly. My kind of town.

It was like looking at myself in the mirror.

Leon King. Second son of Augustus King, the erstwhile emperor of Sydney's crime scene, now answering for those crimes in a maximum security correctional facility…aka prison.

Yeah, the King is dead. Long live the King.

Or should I say 'Kings'?

The new Kings of Sydney were me and my two brothers, Ajax and Xander, and it wasn't our father's old empire we wanted to inherit, not when we were the ones who'd toppled it in the first place.

No, we were after redemption. Making good on the King name. Building something out of the ashes of the old empire. Going legit or some such bullshit.

At least that was what Xander and Ajax wanted.

Me, I was fine with going legit. Things were a hell of a lot easier if you didn't have the cops interfering with your business, but it wasn't redemption I needed.

I didn't even particularly care about the King name.

I'd been my father's lieutenant, the muscle at his back, and years of dealing out violence to other people had burned the fucks I had to give right out of me.

I'd been happy to be the bad guy back then and, five years after my father had gone to jail, I was still happy to be the bad guy.

It was a fresh start I wanted, in a city where no one knew who I was or who the Kings used to be. Where I didn't have a past. Where I could be whoever and whatever I wanted to be, master of my own destiny. Where I could escape.

But before all of that, I had one last order to obey. A debt I owed to my oldest brother. And I was prepared to do anything to make good on it.

I turned from the view to the sleek minimalist room that was my office. We were in the tower that housed King Enterprises, the hugely successful property development company my brothers and I had formed out of the rubble of Dad's empire.

Hamilton was sitting in the uncomfortable chair I'd positioned in front of my desk. He was an older man, silver-haired and blue-eyed, with that well-preserved look that only the very rich had.

Except he looked every bit of his sixty-plus years right now.

I tended to have that effect on people.

'What do you think I mean?' I gave him my very widest smile, the one that I was infamous for giving right before I was about to do some serious damage; nothing put someone off-balance like a smile right before you punched them in the face. 'I want to marry her.'

Hamilton paled. 'You can't be serious.'

'Of course I'm bloody serious. I'd never joke about the sanctity of marriage.'

He stared at me, confused by my sarcasm and my smile.

Good. Let him stay confused. It would make it easier to close the deal.

'But…why do you want to marry my daughter?'

'I thought I explained.' I adjusted the cuffs of my white cotton shirt, admiring the contrast with the dark blue of my suit and taking my time about it. Small movements right before the gut punch. Another way to play with an opponent, and I did love to play with my opponents. It was such a power trip. 'My brother wants to expand the King portfolio into the luxury apartment market and we're having difficulty getting investors.'

Hamilton nodded. 'I understand that. But I still fail to see why marriage is necessary for that kind of expansion.'

'It's the name,' I said. 'No one wants to put money behind a King. Not with our past.'

A muscle twitched in the side of Hamilton's jaw. 'But you don't need my daughter for that. Simply pay me the money you said you would, and I'll mention to my friends that you're a good bet and—'

'If only it were that simple,' I interrupted with a heavy sigh. 'But sadly it isn't. I need an…insurance policy, you see. In case you decide to renege on the deal or change it, or alter the terms.'

'I would never do that!' Hamilton looked incensed.

I didn't give a shit. He wasn't the do-gooding pillar of the community everyone thought he was, not when he was up to his eyeballs in debts from a gambling addiction he'd tried to keep secret.

Unfortunately for him, it was no longer a secret. At least not to me. I was good at finding dirt on people and I'd found plenty of it on him.

'I don't care what you would or wouldn't do,' I said coldly. 'I need an insurance policy and your daughter is it. Plus, a few "introductions" to your friends is not enough. We need a total image overhaul.' I paused to make sure he was with me. 'Having Sydney's biggest charity donor as my father-in-law will silence anyone who still has doubts about us. And hopefully set a few minds at ease about investing with King Enterprises.'

It had only been five years since our father had gone to jail but people's memories could be long. Ajax,

Xander and I had done very well to get where we were in that time, yet many viewed us and our intentions with suspicion.

We'd gone straight, but in some people's minds we were still criminals.

A past like ours was difficult to escape—and I never would—but I'd do my bit to help my brothers escape.

Hamilton shook his head, but I continued. 'You'll put the word around that we can be trusted. Invite us to all the best charity parties, talk us up to your cronies, tell them the past is in the past, et cetera.'

'You can't possibly think that I'd—'

'And in return,' I interrupted, 'I'll pay your gambling debts.'

Hamilton's mouth closed with a snap, his expression becoming sharper, more predatory. 'Gambling debts?'

'Come now, Tommy,' I murmured, enjoying the spark of anger in his eyes at my patronising tone. 'You're neck-deep in the red at the moment. All those investments you thought would pay off that didn't, all that tax evasion with those wonderful charities that isn't as effective as it used to be. Or maybe you're simply living beyond your means? Whatever it is, I can help.' I gave him another smile. 'All you have to do in return is give King Enterprises the big thumbs-up to your friends. Oh, yes, and your daughter as an insurance policy.'

This time Hamilton's stare was much more assessing, as if he was weighing up a business decision. Which it was: my help in clearing his debts in return for assistance in the image department for the whole King family.

It was a win-win for everyone.

'I have two daughters,' Hamilton said at last, eyeing me.

Interesting. I only knew of the one who featured in all the society pages. Clara Hamilton. A pretty little socialite with a wealth of honey-blonde hair, big blue eyes and gorgeous tits. In other words, exactly my type, and I did like a society girl. It was funny how all their socialite ways would vanish once their clothes were off and I was inside them. How their dignity would crumble as they begged, as I made them scream my name.

On the outside they made a fuss about my past, about my links to my father's crime empire, about all that nasty violence.

But on the inside, in the darkness of the bedroom, they loved it. That past thrilled them, got them off. Those girls loved a bad boy and I was as bad as it got.

Apart from Ajax. He was worse.

'Give me the pretty one,' I said.

Hamilton's mouth twisted. 'Clara isn't—'

'I can't promise I won't touch her, but I can promise I won't hurt her.' I didn't mind a bit of pain with my sex, but I wasn't a fan of forcing myself on anyone. Where was the fun in that?

But Hamilton didn't like it. At all. 'And if she says she doesn't want to marry you?'

'That's your problem, not mine.' I put my hands in my pockets, my posture relaxed. 'Look, it's not a life sentence. Tell her all I want from her is to pretend we've had a whirlwind romance and that she's desperately in love with me. Then we'll have a nice big society wedding and afterwards she can have my

Darling Point mansion. I'll be leaving the country so she'll get it all to herself. In six months, once we've got some solid financial backing, she can send me the divorce papers and we'll both go our separate ways, no harm, no foul.'

Hamilton's eyes narrowed. 'Why the pretence?'

'Appearances matter, Tommy,' I pointed out. 'Which you, of all people, should know. Wouldn't do for it to look like a marriage of convenience now, would it? It's a bit too mercenary. Not at all the image we want for the King name.'

'Divorce so soon afterwards wouldn't exactly project the right image either.'

'It's long enough to convince enough people it's legit and, like I said, bag some investment dollars.' I gave him a conspiratorial look. 'It'll be our little secret, hmm?'

Hamilton leaned an elbow on the arm of his chair and stroked his chin, acting like he was thinking carefully about it. But that gleam in his eye told a different story. He wanted my money and he wanted it desperately.

Perfect.

I remained standing, staying casual. Strange how being relaxed could put people on edge, but it did.

It was putting Hamilton on edge right now. I could see it in the tension in his shoulders and the way he was tapping one foot against the carpet.

I said nothing, letting the silence sit there, because silence could be a useful weapon to someone who knew how to use it. And I did. I was very good with weapons in general.

The silence lengthened, became oppressive.

Eventually, Hamilton shifted then said, 'I'll put the idea to Clara and see what she says.'

I shook my head. 'You do want the money, don't you? I mean, without it, you'll lose everything. And think of the scandal if word got out about your little gambling problem. I don't think you want that, do you?'

He shifted again. 'Fine. I'll make sure she's on-board with the idea then.'

I was conscious of a slight loosening inside my chest, one that couldn't and shouldn't be relief, not when I'd been confident he'd agree to my request, yet felt like it all the same.

Ajax had given me responsibility for securing the King Enterprises' potential expansion and I wanted to make sure I fulfilled that responsibility, especially given what I owed him.

Now it looked like that debt would be paid.

It was satisfying, I couldn't deny it.

What a good little soldier you are.

But not for much longer. Once I was away from Sydney I'd get something I'd always been denied: the luxury of choice.

'You do that,' I said to Hamilton. 'And if she has any issues with the marriage remind her that my house has a pool. Girls love pools.'

Slowly, Hamilton pushed himself out of the uncomfortable chair. 'I do have a condition.'

My smile froze. 'I'm not sure you're in any position to demand conditions.'

'Nevertheless, I have one.' His gaze was very direct and very certain; he wasn't going to back down on this. 'You're not to make contact with her before the wedding. And you're not to touch her after it. It will be a marriage in name only.'

I almost laughed. 'What? You don't want my filthy King hands all over your precious daughter?'

He said nothing, but the look in his eyes was clear. No. He didn't.

I raised a brow, playing with him because that was the fun part and I could never resist a show of power. 'But what if she wants to put her hands on me?'

He flushed. 'She won't. She abhors you.'

'Sure she does. When she doesn't know me from Adam.' I lifted a shoulder. 'Not that I care. Like I told you, if she doesn't want me I won't force myself on her. But if she does...well...' I grinned, just to mess with him '...I can make no guarantees.'

Hamilton's expression became fixed. 'She won't. I can guarantee that.'

It was sweet how protective this pillar of the community was of his daughter. Except, again, I knew it was a sham. It was himself and the reputation of his family that he cared about, like all men of that sort. That and money. I'm sure if I'd offered him more cash he'd have had no problem with me claiming a wedding night from his precious daughter.

Unfortunately, though, telling me not to touch the girl only made me want to touch her even more.

I was perverse like that. Or a cliché—take your pick.

'Sadly for you, not making contact with your daughter negates my need for a public love affair, which means I'm going to have to refuse your condition,' I said, letting my grin fade, showing him steel instead. 'You want my money then you give me the girl. That's all.'

He didn't like that, naturally enough, but, since he didn't have the leverage, all he could do was bluster empty threats as I got Security to usher him out of my office.

As soon as the office door shut behind him I reached for my phone and hit Ajax's number.

He answered with a curt, 'Yeah, what?'

'You'll be pleased to know that Hamilton will give us his backing when it comes to finding investors for the new King Enterprises expansion,' I said.

He grunted. 'How? That prick didn't want anything to do with us.'

'Let's just say I offered him a big incentive.'

'What did you—? On second thoughts, I don't want to know.'

'You don't,' I agreed. 'There's one other thing.'

'What?'

'You need to offer me your congratulations, brother.'

'Why?'

I turned to the view once more, my reflection staring back at me, the predatory smile on my face a reflection of the monster beneath the handsome prince. It didn't scare me, that monster, not any more.

Your bride is going to get one hell of a shock, though.

Yes, she might.

I smiled wider. 'Why? Because I'm getting married.'

CHAPTER TWO

Vita

'YOU'VE GOT TO be kidding.' I stared at my father in shock. 'You want me to marry who?'

Dad had that hard expression on his face, the one he always got when he wanted his own way. 'Leon King, of King Enterprises. The one who—'

'I know who he is,' I interrupted, folding my hands in my lap so he wouldn't see them shake. 'The whole city knows the King brothers.'

Property developers who'd made a lot of money in a very short space of time. Ex-criminals, some would say. Still criminals, said others.

I had no opinion on the subject since it didn't interest me. At least, it hadn't interested me. Not until my father had called me—a shock in itself since I hadn't had contact with either of my parents for about six months—and asked me to come to his downtown office for a meeting.

I hadn't wanted to—I had a report I had to write for my job as a research assistant at Sydney University and the last thing I felt like doing was trying to pretend I still had a relationship with my family. But he'd insisted. Told me it was important. That it concerned my sister.

That I owed them.

He wasn't wrong. I did owe them. In fact, I'd been waiting ten years for him to call in that debt, because I'd had no doubt at all that he would. And now he had it was a relief in many ways.

Except that he wanted me to marry some total stranger in place of my sister.

'Why me?' I tried to keep my voice calm and level because there was no point getting emotional. I'd learned that the hard way. 'Did Clara say no?'

Dad moved around behind his massive oak desk and sat down, giving me the cold judgemental look he'd perfected over the years. 'Not exactly. I haven't told her about it.'

I blinked. This whole thing was getting weirder and weirder.

Odd enough that Dad had called me out of the blue to ask me to take Clara's place and marry some criminal, but that he hadn't even told Clara about it…?

'You're going to have to explain,' I said carefully. 'Because I don't understand how you can not tell Clara. Or even why you're asking me, for that matter.'

Dad was silent, staring at me as if weighing up what he wanted to say.

I stared back. If he thought I was going to fall in line, like Mum and Clara always did, he could think again. Years ago, he'd sent me away to an aunt up north and I'd gone without protest, finishing my schooling away from Sydney society and its far-too-bright lights, burying myself in the relative obscurity of a tiny town and concerning myself only with my studies.

But I wasn't the same person now as I'd been back then. I wasn't seventeen for a start, and I was happy out of the spotlight. In fact, out of the spotlight was where I wanted to stay.

I had a nice, quiet, comfortable life in the labs at the university, completely separate from my family. A life I didn't particularly want to change.

'Fine,' he said after a moment. 'I have some…debts that need to be paid and King has offered to pay them for me. In return, he wants my help with legitimising the King name.' Dad paused. 'And to do that he wants to marry Clara.'

Debts? I shoved that question aside for the moment.

'Why?' I asked. 'How is marrying Clara going to legitimise the King name?'

Anger burned in my father's blue eyes. 'He and his brothers are looking to break into the luxury apartment market and they need investors. So he wants me to get the business community on his side—allay fears about their past, that kind of thing.' Dad said the words as if they tasted bad in his mouth. 'He thinks marrying Clara will help.'

I understood. Though their father had been imprisoned for his crimes years ago, the association still followed his sons around. Not that I knew much about them, aside from the fact that they were notorious for their cut-throat business practices as property developers.

The business world wasn't my world anyway. I preferred science, the quiet atmosphere of the lab I worked in and the comparatively small power plays that were university politics. Not that I involved myself with those either. I kept to myself and I liked it that way.

'I see,' I said carefully. 'It seems an extreme move to marry Clara in order to get a few investors. You can't refuse?'

'No.' The word was flat. 'I need that bastard's money.' He paused. 'It's either that or bankruptcy.'

I stared, shocked. 'Bankruptcy? Seriously? Dad, what did you—?'

'That's not important,' he interrupted. 'The important thing is that he's not going to get his dirty hands on Clara.'

The implication bolted like a small pulse of electricity down my spine, reactivating old hurts, making them echo.

Of course he'd never give up his precious Clara. He's going to sacrifice you instead, the less important one…

I ignored the thoughts. I was over that now. My older sister led a life of parties and social gatherings and shopping, all funded by Dad, but it wasn't a life I wanted. I'd found my place in the lab and I was perfectly happy there. I didn't need him or anyone else to validate me.

'Yet you're okay with him getting his dirty hands all over me,' I commented dryly.

Dad's gaze flickered. 'You're stronger than she is, Vita. You always have been. You'll be able to handle him. She won't.'

Ten years ago I would have lapped up his praise. Nowadays, I knew better. He wasn't praising me—he was manipulating me.

'You're assuming I'm going to say yes.'

His expression hardened. 'You are. These debts must be paid. Including yours.'

It stung, no point in pretending otherwise. He'd always blamed me for what had happened all those years ago, even though, at seventeen, I'd had no idea what I was doing. I'd thought Simon had loved me. I hadn't known he would film himself taking my virginity and put it up on the Internet, with commentary, for his friends to laugh at.

I hadn't known that it would go viral and that soon everyone in the entire world would see it too—including my parents. There had been a media storm and some of the charities Dad did fundraising for and who sponsored Dad's various business activities had withdrawn their sponsorship. Our family had been shamed and embarrassed socially, and it had taken at least six months before people had moved on to the next scandal.

The damage had been done, though. Dad's business empire had teetered on the brink of bankruptcy and it had taken years for him to drag it back.

All because I'd been a seventeen-year-old girl who'd stupidly thought she was in love.

My fault. And Dad never let me forget it.

I looked down at my hands, clasped tightly in my lap. I had no answer to that and he knew it.

'He won't touch you,' Dad said when I stayed quiet. 'All you have to do is go through with the ceremony and live in his Darling Point mansion afterwards. He won't even be there. He'll be leaving the country. And in six months he'll give you a divorce.'

And once you've done it your debt to the family will be paid.

That at least was true. If I did this for my father he couldn't ask anything more of me, surely? I could go back to the private life I'd built for myself. Where I was good at what I did and I was confident in myself. Where I was the one in control.

'You'll get to keep the house, by the way,' Dad added.

I kept my gaze on my hands. The dark blue polish I'd painted on them was chipping at the ends where I'd bitten them, a nervous habit I was trying to break.

I didn't need a house. I lived in a terrace apartment near the university that Dad had bought for me and I insisted on paying the mortgage. My assistant wages were meagre and I was barely able to pay that and cover my living expenses at the same time, but I didn't want any more debts than I had already.

A house in Darling Point, though. You could sell it. Pay Dad back with the proceeds…

No. I would pay my debts myself. My way. With my own money. I wasn't going to depend on anyone else's, no matter how much it was.

Money was never the answer anyway, even though lots of people thought it was. People like Dad.

'I don't want a house,' I said flatly. 'And I don't want money. What I want is my debt to be cleared and never spoken of again.'

Dad sat back in his big black leather office chair and I thought I saw a flicker of surprise in his gaze, as if he'd been expecting me to say something different. 'Okay,' he said. 'If you do this, consider it cleared.'

'You'll stop holding it over my head for good?'

He gave a sharp nod. 'We'll never speak of it again.'

That was something.

You're seriously considering this?

With an effort I managed to stop myself from shifting nervously in my chair, even though fear was winding tight inside me.

No. No fear. No emotion. Marrying a stranger was nothing. Merely a business proposition or an experiment. Or even trying out a new recipe. Sometimes it worked out and sometimes it didn't, but it was nothing to get emotional about.

Nothing I needed to care about.

'Does he know he'll be getting me instead?' I curled my fingers in tight to my palm to stop from lifting them to my mouth and nibbling on the ends.

Slowly, Dad shook his head.

We both knew why that was. No self-respecting playboy would choose me when he could have Clara.

'He'll be angry,' I said.

'He'll have to deal with it.'

Dad's expression had hardened, making the fear inside me tighten, no matter how much I tried to ignore it.

Leon King would be angry. He thought he'd be getting curvaceous and beautiful Clara and he'd end up with…me.

Vita Hamilton. Tall and bony. No curves to speak of. Two aspirins on an ironing board. And those were the kinder things Simon had said about me in his commentary on the video. Other people had rushed in with worse comments about my thick gingery hair. My freckles. And…other things.

I shoved the memories away. My physical appearance wasn't important and I'd been stupid to let all those comments get to me. It was my mind, my intellect that made me stand out and that, at least, I was proud of.

'He might refuse to go ahead with it,' I said.

'He wants those investors, Vita.' Dad's expression was nothing but sure. 'He'll go through with it. Don't worry about that.'

That...wasn't exactly what I was worried about, though I wasn't sure what I was worried about or why I was afraid.

I didn't know Leon King so his opinion of me—if he had one at all—didn't count. All I had to do was say the words, get the ring, live in his stupid house and then it would be done.

No big deal.

Except Leon King was newsworthy, and no doubt the media would be very interested if he suddenly turned up with a fiancée. Especially a fiancée like me.

There goes your nice quiet life.

My heart was suddenly beating fast and my palms were damp and sweaty. I gritted my teeth, reining in my flailing emotions and shoving them aside.

I needed to be cool about this. Logical. Practical. I was a scientist now, not a shamed and humiliated teenager that the entire world had seen naked.

I was stronger than that—much stronger.

There is a way out of this.

An idea opened up inside me like an elegant solution to a difficult research question, or the missing ingredient in a recipe I hadn't managed to perfect.

Leon King wasn't a man who'd appreciate being played the way my father was intending to play him. And he certainly wouldn't be pleased to find out he'd be getting me, not Clara.

But what if I approached him myself and told him what my father was planning? What if I gave him a heads-up? He'd probably take one look at me, realise I was no Clara and decide he didn't want to get married after all. There was the issue of Dad's debts, but maybe he'd simply be happy to have Dad talk him up in return for paying those off. He didn't need to marry me.

It might not work. Leon King was, after all, a notoriously ruthless businessman and I was simply a research assistant. But I was sure I could make him see reason. Once I explained it all logically, he'd understand.

'Well?' Dad said sharply. 'Think of your sister. Are you going to do this for us or not?'

I lifted my gaze from my hands and met Dad's. 'Okay,' I said. 'So, what do I need to do?'

He looked away. 'Nothing at the moment. Just keep your head down until the big day.'

Of course I would.

After I'd let Leon King know exactly what was going on.

CHAPTER THREE

Leon

'SHE'S NOT HERE,' Xander said, his clear, cold voice cutting through the hard beat of the nightclub's music.

I ignored him, looking out over the heaving crowd and trying to figure out which of the blondes on the dance floor was Clara Hamilton. It was difficult to tell since there were a lot of blondes and the dim lighting made their faces hard to recognise.

We were sitting in the VIP area of Red Door, the city's current nightclub du jour, and pretty little Clara was supposed to be here—at least that was what Hamilton had assured me. But, as my younger brother had so eloquently pointed out, she wasn't.

Annoying.

I'd sent Hamilton an email detailing the number of dates Clara and I were to go on, the locations and what would be expected of her in order to make this look real. And he'd sent me a response letting me know that Clara had agreed to my terms and that she'd be there for the first date, tonight, at Red Door.

But I'd been here a good hour already and there was no sign of her.

I was beginning to wonder if good old Tommy Hamilton had lied and hidden his daughter from me. If so, there would be words to be had. A great many fucking words and none of them to his liking.

Xander sat opposite me, stone-faced as usual, his dark eyes glittering as the club's lights flashed. It wasn't his scene—he spent most nights holed up in his office since he was a total workaholic—so I was surprised he'd decided to come with me tonight.

'Do you have a reason for being here?' I asked. 'Or is it to sit around pointing out stuff I'm already aware of?'

'I wanted to meet her.' He didn't look at me, too busy studying the dance floor. 'Make sure she's no threat to us.'

'She's a pretty socialite, Xan. How much threat could she possibly be?'

His gaze met mine. 'Some women are dangerous.'

He would say that since he was currently having issues with our stepsister, Poppy. As in he hated her and she hated him.

I grinned. 'Relax, brother. She's my beautiful bride. Of course she's not dangerous.'

I'd given him the run-down of my plan, along with Ajax, and both of them were on board with it, though Ajax more than Xander. Ajax liked the idea of rubbing our status in the noses of those who'd once been our enemies, while Xander didn't much care. He was all about the money and protecting our investments.

Xander snorted and looked away, studying the dance floor again.

'Have a drink,' I said. 'In fact, have two. Maybe they'll dissolve that stick currently jammed up your ass.'

Ajax would have told me to fuck off. Xander merely ignored me, then, without a word, pushed himself up off the couch and disappeared through the crowd, heading towards the bar.

Good. I could use some time to myself to figure out what to do about Clara's non-appearance.

I sat back on the couch, reaching for the glass of very expensive single malt I preferred and, as I did so, I caught the gaze of a woman sitting at a table near the stairs to the VIP area.

She was staring very hard at me.

Stares weren't unusual—I got them a lot, especially from women—but I never looked back unless the woman was worth a second glance. And this one wasn't.

Yet I found myself looking back now, unable to put my finger on why. She definitely wasn't my type. At all. She wore a close-fitting black dress, more suited to a funeral dinner than a nightclub, that highlighted a body that was all angles and no curves. Her dark hair had been drawn back unflatteringly tight against her skull, making her plain, sharp face seem even more disapproving than it already was.

She looked like an offended nun.

Why the hell was I staring at her?

Christ, I had no idea. Maybe it was the way she was staring at me: intense, direct. No blushing and looking away like some women did, or lowering her lashes and shooting me flirtatious glances from underneath them. No come-and-get-me smiles or looking past me, pretending she hadn't been staring.

No, she simply stared. Then she slid off her stool and headed towards the stairs to the VIP area.

Shit. She was coming up here?

Intrigued despite myself, I watched her make her way to the top of the stairs and talk to the bouncer who was guarding the area. She pointed at me as she did so, an earnest expression on her face and, sure enough, the bouncer glanced at me then headed in my direction.

Interesting. What could this woman possibly want? Other than the usual. But then there hadn't been anything flirtatious or sexual in her gaze. No, it wasn't sex she wanted, I was sure.

'Mr King?' The bouncer came to a stop in front of my table. 'There's a woman here who wants to talk to you. She says it's about Clara Hamilton.'

I stilled. Looked like my evening was about to get even more interesting.

'Send her over.' I glanced past him to where she stood, looking in my direction. There was a crease between her brows that disappeared as the bouncer signalled to her, then she started forward without hesitation.

Keen little thing, wasn't she?

Though, as she got closer, it soon became clear she wasn't little. Tall. Taller even than I'd thought at first and her heels weren't exactly high. She moved with purpose too, as if she knew exactly where she was going and why.

'Mr King.' She came to a stop in front of my table. 'Thanks for seeing me.' Without waiting for me to reply, she held out her hand. 'I'm Vita Hamilton.'

I made no move to get up or take her hand, settling for staring at her instead.

She had dark eyes, almost as dark as Xander's yet without the black hole effect his had. Hers were very bright, as if there were tiny stars dancing in the depths. And she didn't smile, merely pinned me with those dark, bright eyes, her hand held out steadily.

People didn't hold my gaze for long. They didn't like what they saw in it, especially when I smiled.

I stared right back. And grinned.

There was a tiny flicker of response, but that was it. She didn't look away or drop her gaze. Or her hand.

Hell, that was…intriguing.

A woman of determination, obviously.

I leaned back in my seat, raising my glass and sipping again, pointedly ignoring her hand just to be a prick.

A flash of irritation crossed her face. Again, intriguing. People were too afraid to get irritated with me. Instead, they either got embarrassed or pretended whatever I'd said or done hadn't happened.

Vita Hamilton didn't pretend.

'Well.' Her voice was clear and bright like her eyes. 'I was only trying to be polite. You don't have to be rude.'

Was she reprimanding me?

Holy shit, she was.

Without waiting for a reply, she dropped her hand then sat down on the seat that Xander had vacated, opposite me, leaning forward and once again pinning me with that dark, starlit stare. 'Now,' she said seriously. 'Like I said, my name is Vita Hamilton and I—'

'I heard the first time, sweetheart,' I interrupted. 'You don't have to say it again.'

She bristled, her mouth thinning in annoyance. 'I'm not your sweetheart.'

That mouth… If the rest of her was sharp and angular, that mouth was not. It was full and very red and, like a particularly juicy apple, I wanted to take a bite out of it.

Maybe I would. Later.

I lifted my gaze to hers. 'Since you're only here with my permission, you're whoever I want you to be.'

She sniffed, annoyance glittering in her eyes. That was different. Fear was the usual response to me, either that or sexual hunger. But I wasn't getting either of those from her.

How fun. I hadn't had a prim girl to play with in a long time.

'Whatever,' she said, clearly uninterested in flirting or any other kind of chit-chat. 'I'm here to talk to you about Clara. I'm her sister.'

Well, that got me.

I gave her another once-over, trying to see the resemblance. Around the mouth maybe, but that was the only thing about her similar to Clara. The rest of her… She wasn't at all like her pretty, curvy, sexy sister.

I took another long sip of my Scotch. 'Perhaps you could tell me where she is then? She's supposed to be here. With me,' I added, just in case things needed clarifying.

Little Miss Vita didn't blink or look away, which was strange when most people sensed what was beneath the mask I wore of the handsome, charming playboy. They could sense the predator, the shark beneath the surface of the beautiful blue sea. And, whether or not they knew what I truly was, they certainly feared it.

But not this woman. She either couldn't see or sense my true self or…she wasn't afraid.

A bolt of something electric, like lightning, went through me, making me go very, very still.

'I don't know where she is,' Vita said, holding my gaze and not even flinching. 'You're supposed to be marrying her, though, aren't you?'

Was she afraid? Did she really not see me?

I smiled wider, giving her a glimpse. 'And?'

Again, not a blink. All I got back was another flicker of irritation. 'Well, I'm here to warn you that you're not.' She hesitated only a fraction. 'My father is planning on making you marry me instead.'

CHAPTER FOUR

Vita

HE WAS LIKE a big cat about to pounce, and my heart started beating very loud and very fast in my ears.

Leon King was dangerous, that much I'd known from the moment I'd laid eyes on him. Very, very dangerous. And right now he was radiating that danger so intensely I could almost taste it.

It made me want to cower away like a frightened rabbit, but I was a professional woman of twenty-six and there was no way I was going to run so I kept staring at him instead, refusing to look away.

He was probably the most beautiful man I'd ever seen.

His features were strong, with a high forehead, chiselled jaw and cheekbones to die for. His eyes were a smoky amber, framed by thick dark lashes and straight dark brows and his hair was tawny, threads of gold and caramel gleaming in the nightclub's dim lighting. Those flashes of gold looked like someone had taken a paintbrush to him and gilded his features.

He wore a white business shirt beneath his dark blue suit and it was open at the neck, exposing golden skin. And he sat there, all sprawled and lazy like a lion sunning himself on a rock.

A predator pretending not to notice its prey, as it readied itself to lunge.

That amber gaze was on mine and the air of danger around him was so thick I could barely breathe. The primitive fight or flight response was kicking in now, urging me to run, but I ignored it.

It was simply a chemical reaction and, as a chemist, I knew all about those. The danger wasn't real so I stayed exactly where I was, determined to show this rude asshole I wasn't intimidated.

'I think you'd better explain, sweetheart.' His voice was deep and rich and vaguely hypnotic. 'Why is your father planning a bait and switch?'

I ignored the sweetheart thing. He was only doing it to get a rise out of me, I was sure. 'Because he doesn't want you to marry her.' I didn't add the fact that it was because I was more expendable. It certainly wasn't about me being stronger than Clara, that was for sure.

'Uh-huh.' Leon King's stare was absolutely relentless and completely terrifying. The smile that curved his beautiful, sensual mouth even more so. 'You're telling me this, why?'

That caught me off-balance. I thought he'd be angry about it and yet… I didn't see anger in his dark golden eyes. No, it was worse. There was nothing in his eyes at all. Absolutely nothing.

I tried to get my thoughts together. 'I'm telling you because I thought you'd want to know. And because…' I steeled myself '…I thought that if you knew, maybe you'd change your mind about this marriage business.'

'Right.' He said the word slowly, drawing it out.

'This marriage business…' Raising his glass, he took another sip of the liquid, his movements unhurried, as if he had all the time in the world. 'And why would I change my mind?'

I blinked, nonplussed and not sure what to say. 'You wanted Clara. And instead you'll get me.' Surely he'd see he wasn't exactly getting a bargain? 'You can't be happy with that. Anyway, I know you're only marrying her to get what you want for your company.' I leaned forward, keen to make him see reason. 'Which makes it pretty simple. All you have to do is pay Dad the money you were going to and he'll make his friends invest or whatever it is you want them to do. There's no real need to marry her or anyone, in fact.'

'You're assuming that's the only reason I wanted to marry her.' He smiled that terrifying smile. 'But it's not.'

A kind of foreboding settled in my gut.

Maybe I didn't want to know his real reason. Before I'd ventured into the city to find him I'd done a bit of research into him and his background, and what I'd found was every bit as terrifying as his smile.

His father had once run the biggest crime network in Sydney. Guns, prostitutes, drugs… You name it, Augustus King had been into it. And Leon had been part of that network, enforcing his father's word as law. At least until he and his two brothers had taken their father down. They'd been granted immunity from prosecution—likely in return for testifying against their father—and had spent the last five years building up King Enterprises, their property development firm.

He was supposed to be going straight, but that

smile of his told another story. A story I probably wouldn't like.

'Go on,' he murmured when I didn't say anything, watching me from over the rim of his glass. 'Ask me what my other reason is.'

I wanted to refuse, but the scientist in me wouldn't let it go. 'Okay, so what's your other reason, then?'

'I don't trust your father, sweetheart. I need an insurance policy. Something to make sure he keeps his word, if you understand me.' He smiled yet again. I wished he'd stop doing that. 'Clara was supposed to be my insurance policy. Sure, I would have preferred her but…' His gaze dropped, running over me. 'You'll do. Yes, you'll do very nicely indeed.'

At first, I didn't know what he was talking about. Since the sex tape crap had hit the media and I'd hidden myself away, I'd cut men out of my life for good. I'd had less than no interest in them or dating, or any kind of relationship at all in fact.

I had good working relationships with my male colleagues, but I made sure to keep them at a distance. All my colleagues. I didn't want anyone knowing about me. I didn't want anyone interested in me. And for ten years that had worked well.

Yet the way Leon King was looking at me, so blatantly sexual… No one had looked at me like that in a long time, if ever. But what was even worse was the sudden wave of heat that licked over my skin in response. Like I'd been caught in the backdraught of a wildfire.

It was so intense I looked away despite all my determination not to, my cheeks getting hot.

Hell. I was blushing. When was the last time that had happened?

Pretending I was studying the crowd and not avoiding his gaze, I said, 'I don't want to marry you. Insurance policy or not.'

'Why not?'

The question irritated me. Was he stupid? Did he really not know?

I steeled myself yet again to meet his dark golden eyes. 'Why do you think? I don't even know you.'

He gave an elegant shrug. 'So?'

'What do you mean "so"? You're a complete stranger.'

'Why does that matter? Complete strangers marry each other every day.' He tilted his head, the lights striking deep gold from his hair, his gaze gleaming. 'I presume your father told you that you'll get my house. Plus I can throw in some more money to sweeten the deal.'

'I don't want your house and I don't want your money,' I said flatly.

'Sex then. You can have me.' That smile lost its edge, became warmer, which somehow made it seem even more terrifying than before. 'I assure you I'm worth it.'

He was so damn arrogant that I should have laughed. If he'd been another man, I would have. But again that strange heat licked up inside me at the words, a pull deep inside.

Yes, and remember what happened last time you felt that?

Shame. Humiliation. Pain.

No, I shouldn't think of that. Chemicals, that was

all this reaction was. Serotonin. Adrenaline. Dopamine. Nothing more.

'No.' I put every ounce of denial I could into the word, sitting up straight and tall to show him I meant business. 'I don't want you either.'

He laughed, a soft sound that made me shiver. 'Then maybe your poor father doesn't get his money.'

'Why not? You'd really pull out just because I won't marry you?'

He gave another shrug as if it wasn't a big deal. 'I'm not risking my money to your father's promises, not without some guarantee.'

Dammit.

I shifted on the chair then rubbed my temples with one hand. The relentless beat of the music was giving me a headache and this was…not going like I'd planned. I'd thought he'd be a typical man, only concerned with having the beautiful trophy woman on his arm. But apparently he was different for some reason. Which was irritating.

Tell him it's all off. Leave Dad to get out of this one himself.

I could. Except then the debt I owed Dad would still be there, hanging over my head. He'd got me away during the media storm, tried to cover my tracks and get rid of that recording. All the while facing the bankruptcy that I'd caused. I did owe him something.

Leon watched me, his gaze a searchlight uncovering all kinds of things I'd prefer to keep hidden.

'What, exactly, is your problem?' he asked. 'I won't touch you if you don't want me to, and at the end of six months you can have my house and a divorce.

I'll be leaving the country after that anyway. You'll barely see me.'

He made it sound so reasonable. Why was I balking? I didn't have any particular beliefs around marriage and love wasn't real anyway. So what did it matter?

'I don't like…the attention,' I said lamely, settling on the most logical reason for my reluctance. 'I'm not comfortable being in the spotlight. And marrying you will draw attention.'

'Of course it will. I want it to.' His gaze wandered over me again and I felt my skin prickle in response. 'I want people to think we're in love, not that I married you purely to get an in with your father.'

Well, Dad had not mentioned anything about a love affair.

'But that's why you are marrying me,' I pointed out.

'Well, yes. I just don't want other people to know that.'

'Why not? Why should you care?'

He gave another of those soft laughs, his eyes gleaming. 'The King family has changed, Miss Hamilton. We're not the criminals everyone seems to think we are, not any more. And what better way to illustrate that than for one of us to fall desperately in love and marry a good woman from a very good family?'

'Not to mention getting investors for your company's expansion,' I said dryly.

'That too.' He swirled the liquid in his glass. 'It's a multi-layered, complicated problem. I wouldn't think too hard about it if I were you.'

Was that a not-so-subtle dig at my intelligence? 'Not to worry my pretty little head, you mean?'

He shrugged, his gaze guileless, and didn't answer. 'Did you know I was supposed to be meeting Clara for our first public date tonight?' he asked instead. 'She didn't turn up, but you did.'

Public dates? Dad hadn't mentioned anything about public dates.

Because he knew you'd refuse.

'I didn't know Clara was supposed to be here,' I snapped, freshly annoyed at my father all over again. 'Dad didn't mention it to me. And I'm certainly not here to be her stand-in either.'

'Clearly not.' He tilted his head. 'What have you got against a bit of attention, though?'

Great. That was all I needed. To drag up what had happened to me ten years ago. I didn't want to talk about it and I especially didn't want to talk about it to him.

'I just don't like it,' I said.

'Bullshit. Must be something pretty bad for it to involve coming to talk to me personally.'

Dammit. My options were either lying or simply not answering the question, but I was hopeless at lying and I had a feeling he wasn't the type to simply drop a subject.

Hiding it wasn't an option either, not when a quick search on my name would bring up the video. No matter how hard Dad had tried to scour it from the Internet, he hadn't been able to. The Internet was for ever and so was my video.

He'll see it if you tell him.

My jaw tightened. Well, everyone in creation had seen it, so why should I care if he did? Possibly he already had.

'Google my name and you'll find out.' I lifted my chin and folded my hands in my lap so I wouldn't be tempted to bite on my nails.

He gave me a long, silent, assessing look. Then he put down his glass and reached into his pocket, bringing out his phone.

I opened my mouth to tell him that he should wait until I wasn't around at least. But his long fingers were already moving over the screen and a moment or two later he lifted his gaze from the phone and looked at me.

I blushed again, the old feelings of humiliation and shame washing over me, but I shoved them away. I wasn't that girl in the video, not any more.

Instead, I stared, daring him to say a single word.

He merely lifted one dark brow. 'So you had a sex tape drama. Who hasn't?'

Was he being flippant? I couldn't tell.

'But you can see why I don't want any kind of public attention. I don't want anyone dragging that up again.'

'You're thinking about this all wrong, sweetheart.' Casually, he dumped his phone on the table then sat back against the couch, lifting his arms along the back. 'You could hide away for ever, afraid of all that coming back up again. Or you could go for a little revenge.'

It was not what I'd expected him to say.

'Revenge? What do you mean revenge?'

'A hot guy slept with you and humiliated you. And millions saw it. What better revenge than to show those millions of people another guy falling for you? Incredibly handsome, sickeningly rich.' He gave another smile, utterly and completely charming, and not at all modest. 'Notorious. Not a man anyone would mess with. Yet you'd have him wrapped around your little finger.'

The words slid under my skin in a way I wasn't comfortable with. Revenge wasn't what I wanted. Oblivion was, and I didn't want anything to disrupt that. And yet…

'I'd already planned some dates with Clara,' he went on, that rich, deep voice of his winding around me. 'Nothing major, just a few public outings to show people we're in love. And then a big wedding to top it all off.' His voice deepened, became softer. 'Yes, it's attention. But this time you get to call the shots. And it ends with you getting everything. The wedding, the mansion, the money.' He paused, gold glimmering in his eyes, his smile making me feel hot, even though I wasn't. 'And, of course, you get the man.'

My instant response was to tell him no, that I didn't care. I'd got past what had happened to me and what I wanted was to go back to my obscure life and carry on as if none of this had ever happened.

You could do that. Or you could rewrite your own story. And this time with the ending you want.

The thought hit me hard.

Back when I was seventeen, being Clara's tall, gangly stick of a sister had been tough, and I'd longed to be like her. Pretty and curvy, popular with all the boys. I'd been an easy mark for Simon. Desperate for attention, insecure, a prime target for his manipulation. And he had manipulated me. He'd made me think he wanted me, that he loved me.

Then he'd used me, humiliated me, and all because he'd wanted my sister and she'd refused him. I'd been his revenge on her, too naive and stupid to understand what he was doing.

So, in a way, Leon King was right. This would be a perfect kind of revenge. And it would be my choice. Something I could do for myself.

Slowly, I let out a breath and looked at him. 'So… when you say a few public dates, how many are we talking here?'

CHAPTER FIVE

Leon

I HAD HER. Definitely I had her and a good thing too.

Satisfaction swept through me. Yes, Clara would have been preferable and I was pissed off at Hamilton for trying to pull a bait and switch, but fundamentally I didn't much care which sister I married.

It was the marriage itself, the connection to the Hamiltons and the image it projected that I was concerned about.

Vita Hamilton wasn't beautiful. But she'd do.

Besides, the way she'd kept looking at me intrigued me. How she hadn't been afraid and how she'd refused me—and no one ever refused me. Or at least they didn't without risking the consequences.

But she had. And it had been a challenge I hadn't been able to resist.

Five years ago I would have answered that challenge with force. Not physical—not with a woman—but I'd have considered that sex tape information the perfect way to blackmail her into doing what I wanted.

Maybe I would have had to resort to that if she hadn't agreed, but she had. And I had to admit that there was something sweet about her choosing me without the need for coercion.

She sat on the edge of the chair, her head tilted slightly, watching me with those bright eyes. Like a cautious bird or a curious fox. No, definitely more fox than bird with that undercurrent of auburn in her brown hair.

That was fine. She could be a little fox. But there was no doubt as to who the dominant predator here was. Me. And she knew it. I hadn't missed how she'd looked away earlier when I'd let my gaze run over her, or how she'd blushed. And it didn't take a genius to figure out that she wasn't as immune to me as she acted.

'How many dates?' I took another long, slow look at her body to see if I'd get the same reaction. 'I had three or four planned so far.'

The swell of her breasts was tantalising beneath the black fabric of her dress. They were small and round, a perfect fit for my hand. The rest of her was difficult to see from the way she sat, but her legs would be long and no doubt they'd wrap perfectly around my waist. Or drape over my shoulders…

'But they'd be in public?' She held my gaze, determined to show me how unbothered she was by the way I was looking at her.

She didn't fool me, however. Even in the dim light of the nightclub I could see how she was blushing. Christ, did she really think I wouldn't notice?

I watched as the stain of red crept down the delicate arch of her throat to the neckline of her boring black dress. 'Not much point otherwise.'

She shifted on the edge of her chair and at last

dragged her gaze from mine. Her hand half lifted, her finger nearly at her mouth before she put it back down in her lap again. Her nail polish was chipped. A nail-biter perhaps?

'What kind of dates are we talking about?' She gave the crowd a leisurely survey before glancing back to me again. 'Going to the movies? That sort of thing?'

I grinned, letting her know that I'd caught her small nervous movement and how she'd had to look away. That I knew I was getting to her. 'The movies? No, sweetheart. Think bigger.'

Her dark reddish brows arrowed down, the lights in her eyes flickering with irritation. 'Don't call me sweetheart.'

I was definitely getting to her. How satisfying.

'You don't like sweetheart?' I asked mildly.

'Not when my name is Vita.'

'Sure, but you'll be my fiancée. You need a pet name.'

Her mouth tightened. 'I don't want a pet name.'

'Too bad, you're getting one.' I was being a prick, but I hadn't had anyone this delicious to play with for years and I was going to enjoy the hell out of it. 'You can choose which, though. If you don't like sweetheart, your other choices are "baby", "little girl", "honey", "darling" or "sweet cheeks".'

She glared. 'I don't want you to call me any of those things.'

'Hey, I'm all for equal opportunities. I don't mind a pet name for myself. "Stud" or "big boy" is fine. I don't mind "hot stuff". My preference, though, is for "sir".'

Her frown deepened. 'Stop playing with me. I don't like it.'

So. A woman who didn't play games and had no interest in playing them either.

Disappointing. Still, her honesty and directness were refreshing. And, being the perverse bastard I was, they made me want to play with her even more.

Maybe I'd save that for later, though. Now I'd got her agreement to the marriage there was no point risking that for a bit of fun.

'Fine,' I said. 'No games. As to the dates, I'll send you the details later. But fair warning. There will be press involved. My aim is to show the entire world we're in love.'

Another flicker of emotion crossed her face at the mention of the press and it looked like trepidation. Not that I could blame her. I'd only had a cursory look at the first couple of results of that search on her name, but that sex tape looked like it had been a major scandal. Seventeen was a hell of an age for that sort of attention, especially when that attention was the wrong kind.

'But I get to say what happens on them, right?' The trepidation had vanished, her expression becoming more concentrated, fierce almost.

Ah, yes. I had said something like that, hadn't I?

A thread of unease wound through me. I wasn't good at taking orders, never had been, even when my father had been the one giving them. Plus, I hated the thought of relinquishing control of a situation to someone else.

Then again, there were ways around that. Topping from the bottom, and all that.

'Revenge,' Vita said suddenly, as if she could sense my discomfort and was hoping to exploit it. 'That's what you told me. I could rewrite my own story, this time with me calling the shots.'

Shit. Little vixen was good at sniffing out a weakness, wasn't she?

Not that it mattered. It was only a couple of dates, holding hands and some kissing. Maybe more than kissing depending on the situation. And if she didn't want that, then so what? I wasn't attracted to her anyway.

Yet… The devil inside me found her fascinating. It wanted a reaction from her, some kind of response, and I didn't care that she wasn't my type.

I was a predator who wanted the chase and who knew she'd put up one hell of a fight in the end.

'Yes,' I said, already thinking about how I could turn this to my advantage. 'You get to call the shots.'

She gave a nod as if she'd been expecting me to okay it all along. 'All right then. I agree to marry you. But only on the condition that whatever happens in public is directed by me.'

I waved a hand. 'Be my guest.'

'So what happens after the wedding?'

'We'll have a couple of months of blissfully happy marriage so my brothers and I can get as many investors on board as we can, and then I leave the country.'

Her hand lifted to her mouth again, and I was pretty sure it was an unconscious thing because she didn't seem to be aware of it. 'So, I have to live with you?'

'Yes, you'll stay with me at my house—don't worry, it's massive; you can have your own wing. You won't even see me if you don't want to.'

'And then?' She nibbled absently on the end of her nail.

Holy Christ, that mouth. I stared at the full, red shape of it. What if she had those lips wrapped around my cock instead of her own finger? Would she use her teeth? Dear God, I hoped so.

Why are you having fantasies about Vita Hamilton's mouth?

I had no fucking idea.

'Then, like I said, I leave the country.' My voice sounded rough. Jesus.

She tilted her head, dark eyes on mine. 'Why?'

I shifted, uncomfortably aware that my suit trousers were tighter than they'd been two seconds ago. 'Why am I leaving the country? Because I am.'

'Will you come back?'

'No. Hence you getting the house. We'll leave it six months, then sign the divorce papers and you'll be free to go.'

She continued to nibble on her nail, frowning at me, as if she was working out a tricky problem in her head. 'I won't have to do anything I don't want to do, right?'

'Right.' Though I could think of a couple of things I could convince her that she did want to do. Things involving that mouth. I was, after all, very good at convincing people.

'Okay.' Abruptly, she took her finger out of her mouth, much to my relief. 'That's all the questions I have for now.' She reached for the small handbag she'd put down on the seat next to her, obviously getting ready to go.

Except I hadn't finished.

We were in a nightclub and there were a lot of people around and, if I wasn't much mistaken, a couple of columnists from the local gossip websites were propping up the bar. Which made right here, right now a prime opportunity to make our so-called relationship public. Plus, there was a small experiment I wanted to run. Just a test to…confirm something.

'Excellent.' I sat forward. 'Give me your hand.'

She turned her head, giving me a wary sidelong look. 'Why?'

'You're full of questions.'

'I'm a scientist. Asking questions is what I do.'

'A scientist?' Diverted, I gave her another once-over. 'You don't look like one.'

'Really?' Her expression was scornful. 'And what does a scientist look like?'

'Blonde.' I couldn't resist playing with her. 'Big tits. Glasses. Short white coat.'

'No,' she said flatly, refusing the bait. 'Some scientists might look like that, but not the ones I know.'

'Where do you work?'

'In the university, in the labs. I'm a research assistant.' The scorn faded from her voice, a note of pride entering it. 'I have a PhD.' She stared at me as she said it, like she was throwing down a challenge, though what she expected me to say I had no idea.

'Smart, huh?' I refused her bait as she'd refused mine. 'I like a smart woman. You'll have to tell me more on our next date.'

'What do you mean next date? We haven't even had one yet.'

'Sure we have. This is our first.' I reached out towards her. 'Your hand, honey.'

'Not honey.'

'Sweetheart, then.'

'I don't want—'

'Scared?'

Irritation rippled over her sharp little face. 'I'm not falling for that.'

'You know what they say, darling. You have to stand for something or else you'll fall for anything.'

If she could have growled at me she would have, I'm sure.

Instead, she let out an annoyed breath. 'Don't make me regret this.' Then she stuck out her hand.

I didn't hesitate to take it or expect to feel anything when I did. Sure, I'd been fixated on her mouth and had thought about how her legs would feel wrapped around me, but I often thought those things about women. I was a man, after all, and not a very good one at that.

So I wasn't prepared for the shock of raw electricity that jolted me the moment her long slender fingers touched mine. Or to see the same shock mirrored in the wide dark of her eyes.

She went still, the muscles in her arm tightening in preparation to jerk her hand away.

And I had one crystal-clear thought.

No. She wasn't going to do that. Not here, not in full view of everyone. Not when this was the moment I'd chosen to reveal our relationship to the world.

So I closed my fingers around hers and held on.

She took a sharp breath.

Her skin was cool but it warmed against mine, and I didn't think it was my imagination that the lights in her eyes flared briefly.

Yes, she felt this too.

I held her gaze in silent challenge. Then slowly I rose to my feet.

Her gaze was wary, watching me as if I was a dangerous animal she had to keep an eye on. It nearly made me smile.

Yes, keep watching, little vixen. You never know what I might do to you.

Keeping my fingers wrapped around hers, I moved towards the stairs that led out of the VIP area and down to the dance floor, tugging her with me.

She resisted at first but I didn't pause, drawing her down the stairs and into the crowd.

'What are you doing?' she snapped as I stopped on the dance floor, a small space opening up around us, then turned to face her.

'What does it look like?' I gave her another tug, drawing her closer. 'I'm going to dance with you.'

She blinked. 'What? But I… I don't know how to dance.'

Her wariness had been replaced with an adorable mixture of shock and confusion. And that was perhaps why she didn't resist as I put my hands on her hips and drew her even closer, our bodies almost touching.

She was tall enough that I didn't have to tilt my head to look down into her eyes.

'Don't worry,' I said softly, staring into her bright, black gaze. 'Just follow my lead.'

She blinked again and something hot and raw sizzled between us.

We were mere inches apart, the soft curve of her breasts nearly brushing my chest, the heat of her soaking into my palms where they rested on her hips. She wasn't wearing any kind of perfume but I could smell her, a delicate musky scent with a floral hint.

It was delicious. It sent a bolt of pure lust straight to my cock.

Oh, pretending to be in love with her was going to be no hardship. No hardship at all.

I firmed my grip on her and a spark flared bright and brilliant in her eyes, making everything in me harden in anticipation.

I could kiss her right here, right now, and she wouldn't protest. That beautiful mouth would open under mine and she'd taste so sweet, I just knew it.

But…perhaps not yet. It would be better to give her some time to get used to the idea of marrying me, not to mention get used to me getting close. It wouldn't do to come on strong and frighten her away.

We were supposed to be madly in love after all.

So I didn't kiss her. Instead, I let her go. 'Perhaps we'll leave it tonight then,' I murmured, not bothering to explain. 'I'll be in touch.'

I smiled at her. Then I walked away.

CHAPTER SIX

Vita

LEON KING WAS a Grade A bastard.

The day after I'd met him in the nightclub and he'd forced me to dance he sent me a schedule of the dates he'd be taking me on, with times, not to mention the name of the wedding planner who'd be handling the wedding itself. There were dates attached to that too—he wanted the marriage to happen as soon as possible while at the same time generating the maximum amount of publicity.

Four weeks was enough time apparently.

And he hadn't only sent the schedule to me; he'd sent it to my father as well. So now Dad knew that not only had I met with Leon King without telling him, I'd tipped Leon off about me being Clara's stand-in.

Yet that wasn't the worst part.

The worst part was the link Leon had included with the schedule. A link that went to a page on some awful gossip website where there was a terrible write-up about Leon King's new 'love'. A photo accompanied it. A photo of him holding me on the dance floor just before he'd walked away.

I'd tried very hard to forget about the moment he'd held me close, his predator's eyes watching me all the while. And I still didn't know what had happened to me in that second. Why I'd let those big, warm hands of his rest on my hips and that tall, muscled body get close to mine.

It had been like I'd gone deaf, the beat of the music fading away, the crowds disappearing, everything lost in the dark gold of his eyes.

I'd just…forgotten I could move.

I'd forgotten I could breathe.

His nearness had been electric, my skin prickling all over, a strange restlessness coiling deep inside me, a heat that seemed to pool right down between my thighs.

It was as if he'd hypnotised me.

I didn't know what it was in the end that made him walk away, but I was glad of it. Even more glad to get out of that damn club as quickly as I could.

What would you have done if he hadn't let you go?

Nothing, of course. All that physical reaction was simply oestrogen reacting to testosterone, or pheromones or adrenaline, take your pick. None of that meant anything, and I should know since I still had the scars to prove it.

Anyway, the upshot was Dad not being pleased and I had to endure a speech down the phone about how irresponsible I'd been and how I'd put the whole plan at risk. I decided not to bother telling him I'd been trying to get Leon to drop the marriage thing to save us both, listening to him in silence instead then disconnecting the call without a word.

He wanted me to marry Leon King and I would.

But not for him or my sister. I was going to do it for me.

For the last ten years I'd been the one in charge of my life and now that I had the chance to right a wrong that had been done to me, I'd take it. I'd marry Leon, slay a few personal demons and then return to the peace of the lab.

My father could take my so-called 'debt' and go screw himself.

The next date was in a couple of days, which unfortunately left some time for the media to find out where I was and how to contact me, and it wasn't long before the phone calls and emails started.

Dread coiled in my stomach every time I looked at my phone and all the notifications and missed calls, but fear was just another chemical reaction and that made it easy to ignore.

I spent the day of the next date head down in the lab, experimenting with a few new compounds. Concentrating only on that and not on the fact that I would be entering the arena again, the media circling me like wolves, while the lion I had to defeat waited in the centre for me, a hungry look in his eyes.

Luckily it didn't seem like my colleagues had noticed any of the websites carrying the story, so I was able to go about my day with relative ease. But naturally Leon wouldn't let me forget and I received a text in the afternoon from him, reminding me of the date and time I would be picked up.

How he'd got hold of my number I didn't know, but it annoyed me.

That night I put on my black dress again—it was the only halfway decent thing in my wardrobe and I couldn't be bothered dressing up anyway—and did a quick make-up job. I hated spending too much time on my appearance and didn't see why I should take more time on it now.

Leon might want us to look like we were in love—as real as love ever got—but we weren't. It was all fake, all pretend. A show for the cameras. Except that I wasn't very good at pretend.

Leon would be, though, I'd have laid money on it. After all, he was a man with a very dark past, though you'd never know to look at him. On the surface he was all beauty and charm, while underneath lurked something else. Something much darker.

Something that makes you curious…

No. Most definitely not. Curious was the last thing I was about him. The very last.

A car came to pick me up at eight and I got in, refusing to give in to my trepidation about the evening by thinking about a new muffin recipe I wanted to try. I loved baking in my spare time since it was basically chemistry with delicious results. And it worked. Kind of.

But what I really should have been thinking about was how I was going to handle this date. I was supposed to be calling the shots yet I had no idea what kind of shots I wanted to call.

It had been ten years since I'd been on a date and I could hardly remember what one was like. Dinner, a movie and awkward conversation were the only things I could recall. That and the desperate desire to be more like my sister and not the gangly girl that nobody liked.

Hideous in other words.

I forced aside the memory and stared out into the city as the car moved through the streets. We were supposed to be going to some expensive restaurant down by the waterfront and he was going to meet me there.

I wondered what on earth I'd talk to him about because we'd have nothing in common, and then what I'd do if he tried to touch me again. It was disconcerting to realise I had no idea about either of those things.

At that moment the driver unexpectedly pulled the car over to the kerb and I was about to ask him what was happening when the back door opened.

And Leon King got in beside me.

I was so surprised that for a second I could only stare at him.

Back in the nightclub, he'd seemed tall—over six two at least—but now, in the close confines of the car, there was no escaping the sheer size of him. He took up all the space with his long legs and broad shoulders, making me feel dwarfed even though I had to be only a couple of inches shorter than he was.

And it wasn't only to do with his height. His physical presence pushed at me, making me want to squeeze myself into the corner of the seat and get as far away from him as possible.

He was so…hot. I could feel the warmth of his body even though he wasn't touching me, and I could smell his scent too. Spicy, like a cedar forest. And I had a weird urge to get close and inhale it, touch his skin to test his heat.

You wanted to do that with Simon too. Remember?

How could I forget? Handsome, attractive Simon.

The first man to pay attention to me. The first man I fell in love with. The man who recorded himself taking my virginity then uploaded it onto the Net, complete with commentary.

The memory was enough to banish the urge to touch Leon King completely, but not quite enough to make me shift away. No way was I going to let him know that he affected me.

'Good evening, sweetheart,' he said, grinning as he pulled the door closed after him. 'Hope you don't mind me dropping in like this, but I thought we should arrive together. Plus, I wanted to give you something.' His smoky golden gaze flashed over me then narrowed as he took in what I was wearing, his grin fading. 'Please don't tell me you're wearing the same dress that you wore to the nightclub.'

Irritated by the effect of his physical presence and unexpectedly stung by the disapproving look on his face, I folded my hands in my lap and lifted my chin. 'Okay. I won't tell you.'

'You couldn't have worn something different?'

'I don't have anything different. Anyway, it's a perfectly nice dress.'

'For a funeral.' He shifted, reaching into his back pocket to take something out of it. 'We need to have a little talk about clothing.'

'No, we don't,' I said firmly. 'I'm the one calling the shots, remember? And if I want to wear this, I will. Besides…' I sniffed '…you're my fiancé and you're supposed to love me no matter what I wear.'

His mouth curled and for a second genuine amusement gleamed in his eyes. It made something in my chest shift and I had to look away, pretending I was smoothing a crease in the material over my knees instead.

'I stand corrected.' There was a note I couldn't place in his rich voice. 'But you need to work on being more convincing when you mention the word love. Especially since we're supposed to be in it.'

'Love isn't real,' I informed him, keeping my attention on my dress. 'Feelings are simply chemicals.'

'Is that so?' He really did sound amused now. 'Well, you might not want to say that where people can hear us.'

'I suppose not.'

'Excellent. Well, keep the dress, but for the love of God, could you not wear your hair like that?'

I bristled. 'What's wrong with my hair?'

'It's a bit…' He stopped, frowning. Then, before I could protest, he leaned towards me, reaching around behind my head and neatly pulling off the band I'd used to secure my hair.

I blinked in surprise, feeling the heavy weight of it begin to uncoil and slide down over my shoulders. 'What on earth do you think you're doing?' I demanded. 'I didn't say you could touch me.'

'You didn't say I couldn't either.' A look of satisfaction crossed his ridiculously handsome face. 'But that's better. Much better.'

'You can't touch me.' I had to fight not to slap him, which only rattled me further since I had no idea why. 'That's my first rule for the evening.'

He only stared at me, perfectly composed, taking up all the space the way arrogant men often did. He wore another beautifully tailored suit, in dark charcoal this time, with a black shirt open at the neck, revealing smooth golden skin.

He was gorgeous, and rationally I knew it. But he didn't affect me physically. To admit that would be stupid.

Testosterone. Dopamine. Serotonin. That was all it was.

'Well,' he said on a long sigh, 'I suppose if you insist. But if I can't touch you, how am I going to give you this?' He lifted the box he'd taken out of his pocket. It was small and black—a ring box.

I glanced at it. 'An engagement ring?'

'Of course. I organised one this week.' He flipped open the lid, revealing a massive diamond gleaming on a platinum band. 'You're going to need to wear something.'

It wasn't just 'something'. It was a ring that must have cost him thousands. And all for a pretence.

'I hope you can return that,' I muttered, staring at the diamond.

'No. It's yours.' He took the ring out, discarding the box then holding out his other hand imperiously. 'Your hand, sweetheart.'

Oh, no. Not again.

I kept my hands firmly in my lap. 'I can put my own ring on, thank you.'

His eyes gleamed and suddenly I knew I'd said the wrong thing. 'Of course you can. But I want to do it.'

'Why?'

'Because I said so.'

My heart began to beat a little faster. 'I thought I got to call the shots.' I had no idea why I was arguing since it would only make things worse. I just…didn't want him to touch me again.

'And you do,' he said easily. 'While we're on the date. But we're not on the date yet.'

'Yes, we are.'

'We're not in public. And we're not at the restaurant. Therefore we're not on a date.' His mouth curved into the same lazy, dangerous smile he'd given me at the nightclub. 'Your hand, sweetheart.'

Protesting more would only make this into a big deal and it was already a bigger deal than I'd intended it to be.

I was being stupid. He was simply going to put the ring on, nothing more. So there was no reason for my heartbeat to speed up, or my lungs to feel like they couldn't get enough air. No reason for a prickle of excitement to race down my spine.

A streetlight shining through the window of the car highlighted the exquisite bone structure of his face, picking up the brilliant gold threads in his dark tawny hair. The same gold that gleamed deep in his eyes as he stared at me.

A challenge.

'Can't handle it?' His velvety voice slid over me. 'Don't worry, I won't bite.' He paused and his smile widened. 'Much.'

Now he's playing with you again. And you're letting him. Idiot.

Annoyed with myself, I shoved my hand at him, inwardly bracing myself for his touch. And, sure enough, I felt it as his fingers closed around mine, a shock of heat, a burst of wild electricity that made me nearly shiver.

I remembered that electricity. I'd felt it with Simon. Only with Leon it was ten thousand times more intense. Which made it ten thousand times more dangerous.

With an effort I managed to repress the shiver and simply stared back as he studied me, clearly looking for a reaction.

I didn't give it to him.

His smile deepened, as if he knew what I was feeling anyway. As if he could tell how hot the tips of his fingers felt against my skin and how badly I wanted to pull away. And how much his touch frightened me.

And not because you don't like it.

Testosterone. Dopamine. Serotonin.

Maybe if you keep telling yourself that you'll believe it.

I ignored the voice in my head, keeping my gaze on his as he slid the diamond onto my ring finger, his fingertips brushing my skin all the way. It felt like I'd been stroked with a flame and it was all I could do not to jerk away.

But I didn't.

He continued to hold my hand, turning it this way and that, admiring the sparkle of the diamond. 'What do you think?' he asked. 'Beautiful, isn't it?'

'It's too big.' My voice sounded thick. 'And it's too expensive.'

'Yes. That's what I wanted. Big, flashy and expensive.' A gleam of gold as he looked at me. 'Like me.'

'I'm not keeping it,' I said flatly. 'I can't.'

He shrugged. 'I don't care what you do with it. It's yours now.' He released my hand, turning his attention to the driver. 'Let's go.'

I felt relieved that he wasn't touching me any more, but the heat of it lingered on my skin like a burn.

And that disturbed me more than anything else the entire evening.

CHAPTER SEVEN

Leon

I TOOK HER to Ocean, one of the most exclusive restaurants in Sydney, with views over the harbour that included the Opera House and the Sydney Harbour Bridge.

I'd wanted us to enter together, holding hands, but she balked at the last minute, making sure those long slender fingers were occupied with smoothing her hair and her dress and fussing with her handbag.

She was nervous and I knew why.

I'd watched her video.

I'd thought I'd better see it since I was marrying her, plus I was curious. So I'd watched it the night I'd got back from the nightclub. The video itself was difficult to find—her father must have paid someone a lot of money to get rid of it—but sure enough, I found it lurking on a dodgy pirate site.

It had been shot on someone's phone, the whole thing grainy and badly lit. But the sound was clear and even though the face of the man was obscured most of the time, the face of the woman was not.

A very young Vita, slender and pale, swamped by her wealth of auburn hair.

The video wasn't long but it was cruel, her lover providing a running commentary about her narrow body and its failings. It was obvious she had no idea she was being filmed. She took off her clothes awkwardly, but her hands were shaking as she did so and not from fear, not when her excitement and passion were obvious. He made rude comments about that too.

The sex itself looked perfunctory and not at all titillating, and her lover made it clear he didn't enjoy it, all the while mocking her painfully honest responses to him in the commentary.

I didn't like that. Didn't like the way he made fun of her, which was strange because since when did I give a shit about anything? Then again, maybe not so strange. I knew what it was like to be at the mercy of someone else.

I should have turned it off then as there wasn't anything else about it that interested me. Except I couldn't.

Her face caught my attention and held it fast.

As her lover touched her, she looked up at him like he was the only thing in the world worth looking at, the only thing in the entire universe worth looking at. Her heart showed in her face, the contents of her soul incandescent in her dark eyes.

When she looked at him she was…beautiful. There was no other word for it.

'I love you,' she whispered to the fucker who'd filmed her, who'd stopped narrating just so everyone could hear her confession. 'I love you so much.'

The video ended there, with him laughing as if that was the punchline to some extended joke.

So I played it again. And again. Wishing I still had a gun so I could shoot the prick in the face, because I didn't like bullies.

It stuck in my head. Made me wonder what it would feel like to have someone look at me like that. As if I was their entire world and nothing existed for them but me.

I wasn't sure why that mattered to me, not when for the last eighteen years it wasn't adoration I had sought but fear. Being dangerous was better than being loved or adored. Being dangerous made you powerful, and when you were powerful you were the one in control.

So by rights that expression on Vita's face should have made my lip curl.

But it didn't. It got to me. Hit me in a place I hadn't realised I was vulnerable. Which was a worry, yet it didn't stop me wondering about it all the same.

I glanced at Vita now as she fussed with her hair, still thinking about that goddamn video. Thinking about that expression on her face, the passion in her gaze. All of that was now hidden away behind those guarded dark eyes. Banished maybe but not excised, I was sure.

Maybe you could uncover it. Maybe you could get her to look at you the way she looked at the prick who filmed her.

The thought came out of nowhere, sending a thrill shooting down my spine.

Arrested, I went still, studying her face.

I could do it. I could make her look at me like that, make her want me so badly she'd think of nothing else. Sure, she'd been less than impressed with me a few nights earlier, but seduction hadn't been top of my list of things to do then.

To be honest, I wasn't sure why I was thinking about it now.

It wasn't like this marriage would be real in any way, shape or form, so there wasn't much point. Then again, it would annoy the hell out of her father. Plus, there was something about the woman that got under my skin.

I definitely hadn't liked my response to her video, not when I'd been expecting to be mildly titillated. Instead, I'd had what could only be deemed an emotional response and I did not appreciate that.

It felt too much like caring—and caring was a great way to lose control of a situation. And once you lost that control you were fucked.

Not that I would. No matter what I'd told her about her calling the shots, ultimately I had the power here. And maybe seducing her would be a great demonstration of that power.

The idea was attractive. Seducing a woman was one of life's pleasures, especially when she threw down a challenge.

Besides, we were supposed to be in love. She might think it was only chemicals, but some chemistry couldn't be denied. Hell, the glow of a well-fucked woman was often mistaken for love.

What if she doesn't want you?

Ah, but she did want me; I'd seen her response to our physical chemistry in her eyes. She might not like that she wanted me, but she did all the same.

Noticing me staring at her, she flashed me a wary look. 'What?'

I gave her a wolfish grin, turning over thoughts of seduction in my head and not bothering to hide it. 'Don't think I don't know what you're doing.'

'I'm not doing anything.' She turned towards the entrance to the restaurant. 'Come on. Let's get this over with.' Without waiting for me to respond, she strode purposefully towards the doors.

She was definitely avoiding getting close to me.

I followed along behind her, not minding one bit since it gave me the opportunity to examine her figure in greater detail than I had in the nightclub.

Not that the unflattering black dress she wore allowed me to see it, but enough to get an impression of a narrow waist and a slight flaring of hips and thighs. I remembered the feel of those hips under my palms that night in the club, their slight roundness and heat. She didn't have the abundant curves of her sister, but there was no hiding the fact that she was all woman.

The maître d' greeted us as we entered the restaurant and it amused me that Vita didn't wait for me to speak. She gave the man my name and booking time as if she was the one who'd made the reservation.

'Of course,' the maître d' said gracefully. 'Come right this way. We have Mr King's table already set up for him.'

I'd requested the best table, one right in front of the big windows that looked out over the harbour. It was in full view of the rest of the restaurant too, so we'd be seen by the other diners. And, hopefully, the press.

I'd put it out discreetly to various different contacts that we would be dining at Ocean tonight and with any luck that would get us a few pictures. Certainly we would once it became known I was having dinner with the 'I Love You Girl'.

That was the name the press had given her.

After the maître d' had showed us to our table he went to pull Vita's chair out for her, but I waved him away and went to stand behind it myself.

She gave me one of her wary looks, radiating discomfort at my nearness, but I ignored her, smiling and pulling the chair out, gesturing at her to sit.

There was a moment's hesitation then she visibly steeled herself and came to sit down.

I looked down at her as I pushed her chair back in, the lights glossing the auburn in her thick, dark hair and making it gleam. I wanted to stroke it, see if it was as soft as it looked, and why not? She was my fiancée. I had every right to touch her.

So I did, letting my fingertips brush the silky-looking strands. I was right—it was as soft as it looked.

Vita stiffened, jerking her head around sharply and giving me a glare. 'What are you doing?'

I put my hands on the back of her chair and bent so our faces were close, an intimate posture. 'We're supposed to be madly in love,' I reminded her quietly. 'Which means you not jerking away from my touch and glaring at me.'

Her dark gaze flickered. 'You're not supposed to touch me.'

'You're my fiancée. It's going to look weird if I don't.'

She seemed to consider that. 'I...guess so.'

I paused, conscious of the people watching us. 'You're going to have to make it up to me.'

'What do you mean?'

'I mean, you need to show the rest of the nice people watching that you welcome your fiancé's touch and definitely didn't mean to snap at him the way you did.'

Again, her gaze flickered. Wariness combined with irritation, and perhaps a bit of fear.

'I watched your video.' I kept my voice low, looking into her eyes. 'I watched the whole thing.'

A tide of red moved over her pale cheeks and the brightness in the depths of her gaze dimmed. But there was no flicker this time. She was brave, I had to give her that.

'Did you?' Her voice was level, though I heard a faint wobble in it. 'Well, thanks for that, but I didn't need to know.'

'There's nothing in that video you need to be ashamed of. You were beautiful.' I didn't know why I was telling her this. Maybe it was all manipulation, to get her to do what I wanted. Or maybe it was simply that I didn't like the fear in her eyes, because I knew what it felt like to be afraid.

Her cheeks went scarlet and she looked down, silky reddish lashes veiling her gaze. 'I don't want to talk about it.'

'So don't. But remember, you were going to show them someone different this time around. You were going to be the one in charge.'

She still didn't look at me. 'I am in charge.'

'No, you're not. You're afraid.'

That got a response.

Her lashes flicked up, her dark eyes meeting mine. 'I'm not afraid.'

'Aren't you?' I stared back. 'If you're not scared,

then why did you jerk away from me just now? And why aren't you hell-bent on showing this whole fucking restaurant how wrapped around your little finger I am?'

Anger gleamed in her expression, which was very satisfying, and that lovely, lovely mouth of hers went tight. She knew I was right and that pissed her off.

Excellent. I'd take anger over fear any day.

But I'd underestimated her.

The next second she reached up, pushed her fingers through my hair and pulled my lips down on hers.

CHAPTER EIGHT

Vita

KISSING LEON KING was a stupid idea and I didn't know what possessed me.

But the moment he'd mentioned that he'd seen that horrible video, where I'd been at my most vulnerable, something inside me had…changed. Hardened.

Naturally he would have watched it. Why wouldn't he? Everyone else in the history of creation had, so the fact that he'd seen it shouldn't make any difference. Yet it did.

He was so powerful, so dangerous, and so very beautiful. Everything that I wasn't. And that made me feel vulnerable.

My physical responses to him made me feel vulnerable too.

I'd been telling myself it was all about the chemicals, but no amount of rationalising made any difference to the feelings that had swept through me as he'd touched my hair. I'd been achingly conscious of his nearness, of his scent and his heat. Of how long it had been since anyone had touched me and how I'd wanted him more than my next breath.

I thought I'd got rid of desire long ago, but it was clear I hadn't. It had only been sleeping. And now he'd woken it.

And his challenge to show everyone in the restaurant how I'd wrapped him around my finger had been the perfect opportunity to show him that I wasn't afraid.

It had also been the perfect opportunity to prove to myself that this really was just a stupid chemical reaction, nothing more.

So I'd reached for him, pushed my fingers into his hair and pulled his mouth down. But the last man I'd kissed had been Simon and that had been ten years ago, and kissing Leon King was nothing like that. Nothing like it at all.

The second his lips touched mine, electricity coursed the length of my body, earthing through the soles of my feet. Intense, powerful and shockingly hot. The heat of his lips a flame brushing me. Scorching me.

I was conscious of everything: his scent and how soft his mouth was compared to how hard and dangerous he appeared; how silky his hair felt between my fingers and how tall he was, bending over my chair.

The kiss had been meant as an answer to his challenge and as proof to myself that this…chemistry was nothing. That it didn't affect me in the slightest.

But it did. And suddenly I was seventeen again. Nervous and excited, and desperate to touch the man I wanted. The man whom I wanted to touch me in return.

A lie.

Remembered shame and humiliation flooded

through me and I pulled away, turning to face the table once again, folding my shaking hands in my lap.

My mouth was tingling, the echoes of that electricity pulsing through me, my heart beating wildly in my chest.

It's not just chemicals, is it?

No, it had to be. Chemicals I understood and could manipulate. I did it every day in my lab. But these… feelings? I didn't understand them and I didn't want them. I hated them.

I sensed him behind me, his presence a hot, muscular wall at my back, and I thought he might say something. But I didn't turn and he remained silent.

Slowly, I raised my gaze from my lap.

His dark gold eyes were watching me from across the table.

Electricity sparked again, a current that raised all the hairs on my body. But this time I pushed the feeling to one side and didn't look away.

The expression on his perfect face was difficult to interpret so I didn't try. I didn't want to know what he was thinking anyway.

'So,' I said acidly, 'are we supposed to sit here and pretend we're having a lovely time?'

His beautiful mouth curled and I felt another spark light up inside me. I'd kissed that mouth. Me. Gangly, ginger, two-tablets-on-an-ironing-board Vita.

'Yes,' he said. 'That's exactly what we're supposed to do. Why don't you tell me about your job at the university? You said you were a research assistant. What are you researching?'

Ugh.

I tried to think of an alternative topic, but my mind had gone blank and I couldn't think of a single thing.

I fiddled with my napkin to stop myself from lifting a finger to my mouth and nibbling on it. 'It's difficult to explain to a layperson.'

'Try me.' His voice was level yet I had the impression that he hadn't much liked being called a layperson.

I frowned at him, trying to work out why he wanted to know. 'Do you have a postgraduate chemistry background?'

Once again that smile flicked. 'No.'

'Did you study science at university?'

'I didn't go to university, sweetheart.'

'What about high school? Did you do any science at high school?'

'My schooling was…patchy, let's say.'

A hint of curiosity caught at me. Did members of crime families even go to school? Not that I wanted to know. I wasn't interested in him in the slightest.

'I'm not sure I can explain it to you in that case,' I said firmly. 'You need a science background to understand it.' Then, before he could argue the point, I asked, because men did like to talk about themselves, 'Why don't you tell me more about why the Kings are expanding into luxury apartments?'

He stared at me for a long moment. Then he gave a soft laugh and sat back in his seat. 'Fine. We can talk about me if you like, though it's my brother Ajax who heads King Enterprises, and the luxury apartment market is his idea.'

'So what exactly is your role?' I asked, curious.

A glitter of some emotion I couldn't interpret flickered in his eyes as another of those dark, dangerous smiles curved his mouth. 'I'm the PR boy. I get people to see things Ajax's way. It's not so different from what I used to do five years ago, but nowadays I do it with a lot less blood.'

I could see he'd meant it as a joke, but the reminder of his past caught at me, hooked into my curiosity at the same time as it made me uncomfortable. What exactly did he mean by 'a lot less blood'?

I wasn't sure what to say, but luckily the waiter arrived with menus so I was granted a brief respite.

Leon decided on some wine and then there was a brief discussion about food. I wasn't hungry, but I picked something at random from the menu.

A few minutes later, the wine brought and served, we were alone again.

'You're curious, aren't you?' Leon's voice was soft. 'About my past.' He was looking at me with that lion's stare, a silent challenge. 'You can ask. I don't mind talking about it.'

'No, thank you,' I said firmly. 'I'm not curious.'

'Liar.' He lifted his wine glass in his long, tanned fingers and idly swirled the liquid around in it. 'Of course you are. But you don't want to ask about it, do you? Why? Does the thought make you uncomfortable? Does violence make you squeamish?'

I watched that dark gleam in his eyes. It looked like anger, which was odd. Did he really want to talk about that? Or was he simply pushing to get a reaction out of me?

'Not really.' I kept my tone neutral. 'Maybe we should spend more time getting to know one another before we talk about your criminal past.'

The gleam in his eyes became molten and for a second I wondered if I'd said the wrong thing, my heart squeezing in my chest as the tension pulled tight between us.

I saw a movement out of the corner of my eye and a flash.

A camera. Which meant there were press. Which meant people had noticed us. They'd noticed me.

I don't know why I hadn't thought about it earlier—perhaps I'd been too busy worrying about Leon. Now I was all too aware of the purpose of this date: to show the world that we were a newly engaged couple who were deeply in love.

The thought made my entire body go cold.

It was all going to get dragged up again, wasn't it? They knew my name and soon the media interest would intensify. And no doubt my video would start doing the rounds again. I could see the headlines now: The Return of the 'I Love You Girl'!

'Hey.' Leon's quiet voice somehow cut through the icy panic that was winding slow fingers through me. 'Look at me.'

It was a command, the note of absolute authority in the words making me obey him before I realised what I was doing.

I met his gaze, felt the jolt as his focus zeroed in on me.

'Don't give them anything.' The words were low, fierce. 'Don't give them your fear or your anger. Don't let them see it. They don't deserve it. This is your story, remember? You get to decide how it goes, not them. You're the "I Love You Girl" and this time you're getting your happy ending.'

How he knew what I was thinking I had no idea.

I had no idea why looking into his amber gaze or hearing the insistent note in his dark, rich voice felt reassuring either.

Yet it was.

And he was right. This was my story and rewriting it was why I'd chosen to do this in the first place. And all those people watching, all the media waiting, would have to follow my lead.

I reached out across the table towards him, not really knowing what I was doing. But he seemed to, his fingers twining with mine on the white tablecloth.

Electricity seared me at his touch, but I didn't let go. The gold in his eyes felt strangely like a lifeline, as if with one moment's inattention I'd drown in the panic that ran like an icy current through my veins.

His thumb found my palm and he began to stroke it, a slow back and forth that made my breath catch and the light glitter on the flashy diamond on my finger. 'So,' he said softly, 'you've got a very rich, very dangerous and possibly criminal man at your mercy. How does the rest of the story go, sweetheart?'

CHAPTER NINE

Leon

IT WAS THE FEAR in her bright eyes that got to me, because I knew what that felt like. It had been years, yet I could still remember the bitter taste of it on my tongue. To be afraid, to be someone's target.

To be powerless.

I didn't want that for her. Not now, not here. And definitely not when her focus should be on me.

Her palm was very soft where I stroked it, her skin warm. And her gaze was pinned to mine as if I was the only thing standing between her and certain death.

It was…intoxicating.

People usually looked at me with either fear or, depending on who they were and what kind of emotion I wanted from them, longing.

No one looked at me as if I could save them.

Unwanted emotion shifted in my chest and I knew I should let go of her hand, ignore the need to help her. But I couldn't do it.

She was bringing back memories I thought I'd left behind long ago. Memories of being terrified and powerless and utterly at someone else's mercy.

I'd only been fifteen when Thompson, an enemy of my father's, had taken me. I'd been a kid, caught up in my father's shitty, dirty world, and I'd paid the price for it. In blood. Christ, I even had the scars to prove it.

This wasn't the same situation, obviously, but I'd learned how to protect myself. Ajax had shown me. He'd taught me how to be the predator rather than the prey, the hunter not the hunted.

Looked like Vita could have done with the same lessons.

'How does the story go?' Her voice was faint and husky-sounding. 'I don't know how to—'

'Keep looking at me.' I ran my thumb over her palm again, making sure I had her attention. 'Don't think about them. Think about the fact that I'm sitting opposite you, desperately in love with you. You have the power this time. You get to control what they see. So what are you going to do? How are you going to show them that the "I Love You Girl" has moved on?'

She took a breath, her gaze searching mine as if I had the answers she was looking for.

Luckily for her, I did.

'Put your other hand under the table,' I murmured.

'What?'

'Do it.'

Slowly, she did so and I reached for it with my free hand. I kept stroking her palm where it rested on top of the table, while underneath I twined my fingers with hers and drew them to rest on my thigh. Then I held them down.

The table wasn't very wide so she didn't have to lean far, but she stiffened as she touched me.

'What are you doing?' She sounded shocked.

'I'm going to show you something.' I began easing her hand further up my thigh. 'I'm going to show you exactly how much power you have.'

'But I—' She broke off as I pressed her palm down over my fly, her eyes going wide.

The heat of her hand seeped through the wool of my trousers, her touch electric, making my pulse race.

Tension held her arm rigid, but I didn't let her go and I didn't look away.

'Feel that?' I pressed her palm down harder. Fuck, I liked her touching me and apparently so did my cock. 'That's me getting hard for you.'

Colour crept into her cheeks, which was better than the pale look that had been there before.

'No one can see,' I went on. 'No one knows you've got your hand on my dick and that you're making me hard, but you know. You've got the power, sweetheart. You've got the power to make me lose my mind right here in front of all these people.'

She said nothing, her eyes dark as a midnight sky and studded with stars.

I knew I was overstepping the mark here and had no idea what she'd do in response. But then boundaries had never been my thing and I did like to live dangerously.

It was risky to give her the control like this too—something I always kept hold of, both in the bedroom and out of it. But she needed some guidance. And it wasn't like I'd actually lose it.

No other woman had managed that so there was no reason this one should.

Then again, her palm was very warm and I was

getting harder. Christ, I hadn't got laid in over a week and my damn dick was desperate for some action.

I considered unzipping my fly and dragging her hand inside my boxers, getting her to wrap those slender fingers around my cock. But me being insistent wasn't the point. Showing her what kind of power she had was.

So instead, I removed my hand from over hers, making it plain to her that she had a choice. She could choose to pull back or she could choose to keep her palm right where it was. The power was with her.

It was disturbing how much I hoped she'd leave it where it was.

A second passed. Neither of us spoke, and I was ready for her to jerk her hand from my crotch.

But she didn't.

And, just like that, I couldn't breathe, all my awareness narrowing to the warmth of her palm over my fly, the slight pressure of it settling on my aching dick.

Our other hands were still linked on the table-top but I'd stopped stroking her palm and was now gripping her fingers with more force.

Jesus, the feel of her hand and the wide-eyed way she was looking at me were affecting me more than I'd expected. And I wasn't sure I liked it. Yet I couldn't be the one to pull away, not now. Not after I'd made such a fucking performance of giving her the power.

Her cheeks were a deep rose and her hand on my crotch moved. But not away. Instead, she began to carefully explore my hard-on through the wool of my trousers.

The lightness of her touch and the hesitant way she

touched me, all cautious and wary, was so fucking hot it stole the remaining breath from my lungs.

She was looking very serious, a crease between her reddish brows, as if my cock was a problem she needed to solve or a puzzle she couldn't quite figure out.

I'd never had a woman touch me the way she was touching me and I had no idea why that was the hottest fucking thing I'd ever experienced, but it was.

'How is this going to go, sweetheart?' My voice had got rougher but I made no effort to smooth it out or hide the hunger I knew had to be burning in my gaze. She had to keep her attention on me and only seeing what she was doing to me was going to do it. 'You want to jerk me off right here? Make me come in front of everyone in this restaurant?'

The bright lights in her eyes flared. Under the table, her thumb brushed slowly over the head of my dick and I jerked in my chair, the sensation electric.

She noticed and her mouth opened in surprise. 'That's...me?'

Of course it was her. Did she really have no idea?

Stupid question. She was gazing at me with amazement, even a touch of wonder. So no, she had no idea. No idea at all.

The desire inside me changed, became something thicker, hotter.

Women looked at me with lust, but never with wonder. As if I was a brand-new discovery they'd made and were excited and curious about. Or a puzzle they couldn't wait to solve.

No, women loved the orgasms I gave them, but it wasn't me they were interested in. Which was fine and exactly what I wanted. Yet this, now, with Vita...

You need her to stop touching you.

Ridiculous thought. I wasn't so far gone that a hand job under the table and the look on a woman's face would undo me. Sure, I'd given her the control, but I was still master of myself.

'Yes,' I said through gritted teeth. 'That's all you.'

The contained, slightly stern look had gone from her expression and the stars in her eyes were dancing. She looked amazed. Christ, the way she was looking at me, the way she was touching me… It was hot. Fucking hot.

'But I…' She stopped, frowning. Then made another cautious pass over the head of my cock with her thumb, watching me intently as she did so.

I hissed as a bright flare of pleasure licked up my spine and, for the briefest moment, one corner of her mouth curled. As if she was pleased with herself.

And immediately I knew that if she didn't take her hand off me I was going to go over, haul her out of her seat and find somewhere private where I could show her exactly how pleased with herself I could make her.

'Sweetheart,' I forced out. 'In about five seconds this particular story is going to end with me coming all over your hand. So, if you don't want that, I suggest you stop touching me.'

Her eyes went round, the colour in her cheeks creeping down her neck. 'But what if…? What if I wanted to keep touching you?' Her voice got lower, huskier. 'In front of all these people?'

Fuck. She'd taken the control I'd given her and she was bloody running with it.

Little vixen.

But that was my fault. I had given it to her, after

all. I simply hadn't realised how it would affect me. How she would affect me.

'Then you'd better be prepared for the consequences, hadn't you?' I didn't bother to hide my own hunger. 'I hope you're ready for them.'

She didn't look the least bit chastened. Instead, the crease between her brows deepened. Then she ran that goddamn teasing thumb down the length of my increasingly desperate dick and I had to jerk my hand away from hers on the table-top before I crushed it, slamming my palm down as another burst of pleasure shot through me.

The glasses jumped, the cutlery rattling.

Fucking hell. She was killing me.

'Vita.' Her name came out in a growl, my fingers gripping onto the tablecloth. 'Seriously, darling. I'm not joking.'

Neither was she, that was obvious. The pale, scared look had vanished from her face, the darkness of her eyes intensifying, studying me as if she had me under a microscope.

I brought my hands to the arms of my chair, ready to push myself out of it. Ready to do what I'd promised and haul her out of there.

But then the waiter returned with our food and Vita snatched her hand from my crotch, her cheeks going from rosy to scarlet.

I didn't know whether to be relieved or order her to put her hand back where it had been.

She didn't look at me as the waiter presented her with her food, her attention on her plate while I tried to slow my heartbeat and subdue my raging hard-on.

An impossible task.

I couldn't stop thinking about pushing her up against the nearest wall, ripping that awful dress off her and burying my cock deep inside her. Thoughts that weren't exactly conducive to entertaining dinner conversation.

Christ, I'd never not been able to think of something to say, yet now I couldn't think of a single thing. It was like the damn woman hadn't only stolen my breath, she'd stolen half my fucking brain too.

Vita picked up her cutlery, not saying a goddamn word. And I was still so fucking hard I ached.

It made me furious.

How dare she get under my skin? How dare she play with me, get me hard, nearly make me lose it in public? How dare she take the control from me so completely I didn't know how to fucking breathe, let alone what to do with myself?

So I did what I normally did in these situations. I took back the control.

Shoving my chair back, I got to my feet.

Her head jerked up, her fork lowering, surprise crossing her face. 'Where are you going?'

I was already moving around the table, grabbing her elbow and pulling her to her feet. Her fork clattered onto her plate. 'Leon,' she said breathlessly. 'Wait. What are you—?'

I looked down into her flushed face, making no effort to hide my anger or the desire that was eating me alive. 'I told you there would be consequences.'

Then, without waiting for her to reply, I strode from the restaurant, dragging her along with me.

CHAPTER TEN

Vita

I STUMBLED HELPLESSLY after Leon, his grip on my arm firm enough to make pulling away difficult.

Not that I could have anyway.

My brain wasn't working right. I was still struggling to process what had happened when he'd drawn my hand beneath the table and got me to touch him. What I'd felt when he'd put my fingers on his fly. Long, thick…

He'd looked at me as he held my hand down, the hungry gold glitter in his eyes making it plain he hadn't been lying when he'd said I was making him hard.

The skinny, unattractive 'I Love You Girl'. Gangly, ginger Vita.

Me. Me.

I knew I should have taken my hand off him when he'd released it, but the shock of discovery had held me fast. I'd wanted to feel for myself whether it was actually true, whether it was really me doing this to him or…

But there couldn't have been anyone else. He'd

looked at me the entire time and when I'd moved my hand on him I'd seen the flare in his eyes; felt him shudder and jerk; felt him get even harder.

He hadn't been lying. It was me doing that to him. And in that moment all I'd felt was amazement. That my touch could affect him, could make him want me.

He's a man. Any woman's hand on his crotch would have made him hard. It's not you.

Doubt whispered in my head, making me stumble, but Leon didn't pause. He didn't even slow. He pulled me out into the foyer and around a corner to where a short corridor led to the bathrooms.

Then he shoved me up against the wall.

I struggled to breathe, my heartbeat thudding, an unfamiliar excitement coiling in my veins. Strange. Shouldn't I be furious at the way he was handling me?

Yet it wasn't fury I felt as he put his hands on the wall on either side of my head and leaned down so we were nose to nose, his eyes burning into mine.

No, definitely not fury. Or even fear.

I was thrilled.

Simon had never looked at me like that. His interest had been entirely feigned and I'd been too young, too naive to understand the difference. But gazing up into Leon's handsome face, I understood now.

He was staring at me as if he wanted to eat me alive.

It's not you.

But it was so difficult to think about that when he was that close, the coiled threat of his tall, hard, muscled body making my knees go weak, surrounding me in his scent and his heat.

'You,' he growled, his rich voice roughened and deep, 'have been a very naughty girl.'

Adrenaline flooded my veins; my pulse was going wild.

I lifted my chin. 'Why? I didn't do anything.'

'Yes, you did. You got me hard. You nearly made me lose my goddamn mind.'

Wonder curled through me. I'd really done that to him?

You idiot. Most men get hard when you touch their dick.

Of course. It hadn't been me in particular, had it?

I couldn't have said why that felt like such a disappointment, not when it wasn't supposed to matter. I wasn't the desperate seventeen-year-old who only wanted to be beautiful and as loved as her sister. Not any more.

I tried to calm my raging heartbeat. 'You would have been hard regardless of who was touching you, Leon. It wasn't anything I did.'

He leaned closer, our noses almost touching, so close I could see the light brown of his irises and the seams of gold running through them. 'You think that happens with every woman I take out on a date? That I get her to touch me under the table then have to stop and drag her out of the restaurant because I'm so fucking desperate?' The raw heat in his eyes shocked me. 'No, little vixen. No, that doesn't happen to me, not unless I let it. And I wasn't planning on letting it.' He shifted even closer, surrounding me. 'Except you did something, and I don't know what it was, but you need to understand one thing. I'm in charge now, sweetheart, and I get to say what happens next. And since you nearly made me lose my mind out there, I'm going to make you lose yours.'

It couldn't be true, could it? Could I have really made this impossibly gorgeous man lose his mind? Simply by touching him?

It was dangerous to believe him, but…I didn't think he was lying.

Excitement hit me, shivering over my skin, and then I finally took in the last part of his sentence. He was going to make me lose my mind?

'No, you won't,' I shot back. 'No one makes me lose my mind if I don't want them to.'

He smiled, slowly and devastatingly sexily, with a feral edge that made my breath catch. 'We'll see about that. I told you there'd be consequences, didn't I? Time to show you what they are.'

I blinked, realising something that I should have before I'd opened my stupid mouth: I'd just issued him with a challenge. And he wasn't the type of man who let a challenge go unanswered.

Helpless anticipation coiled in my gut.

What had I done? I didn't actually want him to touch me, did I?

Leon moved, taking my wrist and raising it to his mouth, his lips brushing over the sensitive skin on the underside of it.

And all I could do was shudder, his kiss burning like a brand, raising goosebumps all over my body.

You should stop him. You don't want to do this. Not again.

I knew that. I knew what the terrible excitement and the ache that began to pulse between my thighs meant. I knew where it led. And yes, if I'd been thinking straight I would have stopped him.

But I wasn't thinking straight. Had a man ever looked at me this way? Like he was desperate? Like he couldn't wait to touch me?

Desire was rising inside me, a desire I thought I'd cut from my life, buried beneath compounds and test tubes and microscopes. Dizzying, intoxicating.

My breath came shorter, faster, my skin prickling and sensitive.

It had been so long since anyone had touched me. So long. And he was so beautiful, everything I'd once craved.

That's why he's dangerous.

Slowly, Leon raised my wrist above my head and pinned it to the wall, shifting his body in closer, making me so very aware of the bare inches that separated us. 'Well?' he demanded. 'Are you ready to answer for what you did to me out there?'

Another shudder shook me. I didn't know why, but I loved the dominant way he was holding me. Loved how caged and crowded I was by all that hard, hot muscle.

I tested his grip on my wrist and his fingers closed tighter. A thrill bolted the length of my spine.

'Yes,' I said huskily. 'But it won't work. A bunch of chemicals won't make me lose my mind.'

Fire leapt in his eyes. Fire that was burning for me.

'You think that's all this is? Chemicals?' His voice was low and rough and soft as velvet.

'Yes, of course. Testosterone. Oestrogen—' I broke off, a shocked gasp escaping me as he lifted his free hand from beside my head and lowered it, his fingertips brushing over my skin just above the neckline of my dress.

It felt like he'd trailed fire over my bare flesh.

'You were saying?' His hand brushed lower, following the swell of my breast, his fingertips finding the hardened tip of my nipple and stroking it through the fabric.

I gasped again as a bolt of what felt like lightning arrowed the length of my body, grounding between my thighs and coiling there in a pulsing, aching kind of heat. 'Oe-oestrogen,' I forced out, struggling to remember what I'd been saying. Something about chemicals… 'Dopamine. N-norepinephrine…'

'That's very interesting.' His finger brushed over my nipple again, sending another electric bolt of sensation down my spine. 'So all you're feeling now is just a few chemicals, huh?'

I could barely make my voice work. 'Y-yes.'

'Easy to resist then, hmm?'

That maddening finger circled my nipple yet again and I inhaled sharply.

God, we were in public. Someone might have heard me and even now be coming to investigate. They'd find us standing here, see his hand on my breast, doing…things to me.

'D-don't,' I said, panting. 'Anyone could come.'

'They might,' he agreed, lazily circling again with his finger, drawing another helpless sound from me. 'But the only person coming will be you.'

'Leon—'

He bent, his mouth near my ear. 'I want to watch you. I want to see you come apart under my hand, little scientist. And you will, understand?'

Pure excitement shot through me, though I had no idea why the thought of him watching was quite so thrilling.

'Why do you want to see that?' I managed to ask.

'Because I do.' His fingers closed on my nipple through the fabric of my dress and pinched lightly. 'Because I want you to lose your mind for me.'

The breath rushed out of my lungs, both at the sharp jolt of sensation and at the ferocity in his voice. I wanted to ask him why that was so important to him but he pinched me again and only a choked sound of helpless pleasure escaped me.

He gave a low, satisfied growl, obviously pleased with my response, and did it again. Sparks scattered everywhere, all over my skin, lighting up every nerve ending I had, making me tremble.

'Do you want to know what it felt like to have you touch me?' He pinched my nipple harder, and I stiffened as a shock of the most intense pleasure streaked from my breast down to my sex. 'I'll give you a hint.' He slid his hand from my breast down my torso, then further, between my thighs. 'It felt like…this.' And he pressed down with his fingertips, unerringly finding my clit through the material of my dress.

It felt so good. Like I'd gone weeks without food and had finally been fed the most delicious meal I'd ever tasted.

'Leon…' My voice didn't sound like mine and I wasn't sure why I was saying his name. Whether it was to get him to stop or to tell him not to, I had no idea. 'I… Don't…'

'Hush.' His fingers circled and stroked, then slid further down as he pressed the heel of his hand against me, the look in his eyes burning me alive. 'It's just chemicals, little vixen. And they're making you wet for me, aren't they? I bet if I touched your pussy right now it would be all slick and hot.'

The raw way Leon said the words, with an undercurrent of rough heat, wound around me and pulled tight.

He was right. I was wet for him and if he pressed any more firmly between my legs he'd soon find out exactly how wet I was.

His hand rocked against me, an exquisite pressure, and I couldn't stop my hips from moving with him, trying to chase the friction.

Voices drifted from out in the foyer, people either arriving or leaving the restaurant. So close.

'Ignore them,' he ordered, soft and dark, as if he could read my mind. 'Pay attention to me.'

'But I…' I faltered as the heel of his hand found a new rhythm, grinding against my clit, a white flash of pleasure nearly stopping my breath.

Pressure was building, relentless and inescapable.

You're going to lose it.

I said his name again, oddly panicked, as it built and built and built, reaching down with my free hand to pull his away, but he grabbed it and brought it up over my head, pinning both my wrists there with powerful fingers. Then he went back to touching me, stroking me, grinding against my sensitive clit until I was panting and writhing against the wall, helpless against the rising pleasure.

His head dipped further, his mouth brushing over mine. A light, agonisingly gentle kiss.

I was shaking now, the pleasure impossible to resist or contain.

It was going to happen. He was going to make me come, right here, right now.

There were people so close, but they didn't seem important any more. Because he lifted his head, his golden eyes filling my vision, letting me see the hunger burning in them.

Hunger for me.

'Come, Vita,' he said very quietly, pressing his thumb down on my clit. 'Come now.'

And the pleasure detonated like the sun going nova, bright and blinding, an explosion of heat and flame. Searing me. Burning me to ash.

A cry burst from me but Leon bent and covered my mouth with his, silencing me. Then he stood there, his body both blocking me from sight and holding me up as the aftershocks tore through me. Preventing me from sliding down the wall in a boneless heap.

I didn't know how long I stood there, trembling against him as I recovered from the effects of the orgasm, the heat and scent of his body comforting for reasons I couldn't have named.

At last he took his hand away from between my thighs, smoothing down my dress then hooking a rogue lock of hair behind my ear. He stared down at me, the look on his face impenetrable. But gold smouldered in his eyes like a banked fire.

'Time to go,' he said roughly. 'Before I fuck you right here against the wall.'

Heat tore through me and for a moment all I could think about was what it would be like to have him push my dress up and take me with people only just around the corner.

He must have read my mind because he gave me another of those feral smiles. 'Look at me like that again and I might just do it.'

What if I want you to? my brain whispered silently.

And maybe he heard it because his smile deepened.

'Later,' he said. 'And that's not a threat. It's a promise.'

CHAPTER ELEVEN

Leon

'WHAT'S WITH ALL the dating bullshit, Leon?' Ajax's deep voice on the other end of the phone sounded pissed off. 'She's hardly your type.'

I surveyed the view from my seat in one of Sydney's most exclusive rooftop bars down on The Rocks. Yet another vista of the harbour, my favourite theme.

'It's not bullshit,' I said. 'And what would you know about my type?'

'Big tits. Beautiful. Blonde. Am I getting warm?'

An image from a couple of nights ago, of my date with Vita at the restaurant, flickered in my memory. Her, pressed against the wall, cheeks flushed with pleasure, shuddering under my hand. My stern little vixen had thought she could hold out against me, but I'd taken her apart all the same.

'You're not warm,' I told him. 'And she's exactly my type. Anyway, what the fuck do you care whether I'm dating or not?'

'I don't want you losing focus. We need this expansion to happen.'

'I realise that.' I kept my voice neutral. 'And it will

happen. Hamilton's already organising something as a way to introduce us around. As to the dating, it's necessary to make this marriage look real. I told you that.'

'Remind me why the fuck that's necessary?'

'Because I don't want it getting around that the Kings are paying for legitimacy.' I leaned forward, picking up the tumbler of Scotch that was sitting on the low table in front of me. 'What the hell is the matter with you? You're grumpy as fuck.'

'Nothing,' he said. 'Just remember what you're doing this for.'

The call disconnected abruptly.

I sighed and tossed the phone down on the white couch cushions beside me.

Like I'd ever forget why I was doing this. It was for him. For what he'd done for me after I'd nearly been broken by the kidnap and torture that I'd gone through at fifteen. He'd taught me how to protect myself and for that I owed him.

He'd get the expansion he wanted, plus the redemption of the King name. All of which would be accomplished through Vita.

Anticipation tightened in my gut at the thought of her.

I'd planned this second date meticulously. We'd spend some time at the bar out in public, making sure we were seen enjoying each other's company. Then we'd go back to my city penthouse, where I'd deal with this insane sexual attraction once and for all.

Christ, at that restaurant I'd wanted to lift her up against the wall and fuck us both into insensibility regardless of who might have been watching. But that would have undermined the way she'd surrendered to me so beautifully.

Instead, I'd taken her back into the restaurant and forced myself to sit through the rest of our meal. I'd barely been able to concentrate on her awkward attempts at conversation, too busy trying to master my raging hard-on. And when I'd finally dropped her back home I'd never been so relieved to see the back of a woman.

Tonight, though, I'd deal with our sexual attraction where and when I chose. And one little scientist feeling her way around my dick and talking about chemicals was not going to get to me. I wouldn't let her.

I glanced down at my watch. She hadn't wanted a pick-up tonight, telling me she'd make her own way to the bar, and I'd let her have that little bit of control and distance. Because she sure as hell wasn't going to get any of either once she got here.

I was in the middle of looking through some of the gossip websites, noting the reports on the 'unexpected and scandalous' love affair between the notorious Leon King and the 'I Love You Girl'—aka Thomas Hamilton's forgotten daughter—when I heard a hesitant footstep near my table.

I knew it was her even before I caught her scent. She hadn't been wearing perfume the last couple of times we'd met, and she wasn't now, but still I recognised the delicate hint of feminine musk that told me she was near.

Lowering my phone, I looked up.

She stood near the table, holding a little black leather handbag protectively in front of her like a shield. She wasn't—thank Christ—wearing the black dress tonight, but a green silky-looking one with narrow straps that wrapped deliciously around her narrow body, showing off her slender frame.

I stared openly at the way the fabric cupped her small, round breasts and pulled in at her waist, clinging to the slight roundness of her thighs.

Jesus, the more I saw of her, the gladder I was that she and not her sister had been given to me. Because Clara would never have looked at me the way Vita did. Nervous, wary, yet deep in her dark eyes hunger burned. Hunger that only I could feed.

I rose, slid my phone into my pocket and closed the distance between us before she could move.

Her eyes went wide, her lovely mouth opening, but by then I'd settled my hands on her hips and pulled her towards me.

I didn't wait, lowering my head and taking her mouth like I had every right to it. Because, as far as the rest of the world was concerned, I did have every right to it.

But I also wanted to let her know that I hadn't forgotten what had happened between us at the restaurant. And that this particular evening she would be at my mercy.

She stiffened but I didn't stop. Lifting a hand, I ran my fingers along her delicate jaw before letting my thumb trace the underside of her soft bottom lip, then pressing it down, encouraging her to open for me.

She shuddered, a soft moan escaping. Her lips parted and I swept my tongue into her hot mouth, sliding my hand behind her head, pushing my fingers into the softness of her hair and holding her where I wanted her. Then I began to explore her, kissing her hot and deep and slow.

She'd given me a taste back in the restaurant, but that had been so brief it may as well not have happened.

Not this time. This time I wanted her to know she'd been kissed—and kissed thoroughly. By me.

I tightened my grip in her hair, tugging her head back so I could kiss her more deeply, her body arching into mine. She tasted like heaven, like strawberries on a summer's day. And her body was melting against me, all those sharp angles softening in surrender.

Little vixen was passionate and sensual, as I'd known she would be. She kept it all locked up inside her but it was there; I'd seen it in that video of hers. I'd seen it again as I'd held her up against the wall in the restaurant too, and now I wanted more.

My cock was getting hard, liking that idea, and I debated whisking her out of the bar and back to my penthouse immediately. But that would be giving in to my impatience, and right now I needed to be in control of it. We also really needed more time to cement our relationship in public.

I lifted my mouth from hers, relishing the flush in her cheeks and the way she leaned into me, as if she wanted more too. Her already dark brown eyes had gone even darker, making the brightness that glowed in the depths of them more apparent. She stared at me then took a sharp breath and stepped back, clutching her handbag, clearly trying to put some distance between us.

I didn't let her.

Grabbing her hand, I drew her towards the couch then pulled her down onto it with me.

'Smile, sweetheart,' I murmured as she stiffened yet again. 'Remember who you are.'

She blinked rapidly, her lovely mouth curving into a fake-looking smile. 'You could have warned me before you kissed me,' she said through gritted teeth. 'It took me by surprise.'

'We're engaged, which means you're not supposed to need a warning.'

'Yes, but—'

'You kissed me back, Vita,' I pointed out.

'I'm supposed to kiss you back.' She sounded exasperated. 'It was just for show.'

If that wasn't a challenge, I didn't know what was.

'That night in the restaurant, when you came up against the wall, was that just for show too?'

She went pink, the colour contrasting beautifully with her green dress. 'I'd hoped you'd forgotten about that,' she muttered.

'Forgotten?' I lifted a brow. 'Seriously? Sweetheart, all I've been thinking about for two days straight is your hand on my cock. That and making you come again. This time with me inside you.'

Her colour deepened. 'Why?'

'Why do you think?' I let her see the hunger in my stare. 'You started something back in that restaurant and I want you to finish it.'

The green silk across her breasts pulled tight as she inhaled. The colour was lovely on her, bringing out the creaminess of her skin and contrasting beautifully with the auburn of her hair. Tonight she had it falling in soft waves down her back, all shining and glossy in the light of the bar.

She swallowed and I found my gaze drawn to the movement of her throat. It was pale and graceful. I wanted to put my teeth on it, to mark it.

'You don't need me,' she said, looking away. 'There are plenty of other women who'd give you what you want.'

I frowned. She'd said something similar at the restaurant, hadn't she? 'There are,' I agreed. 'But I don't want them. I want you.'

'Why?' Her gaze came back to mine, sharp as a knife. 'I'm not my sister, if that's what you're thinking.'

I didn't quite understand. Of course she wasn't her sister; any fool could see that. 'I don't think you're your sister,' I said. 'And I don't care about her anyway.'

'You wanted to marry her, though. You asked for her.'

Understanding began to filter through. Was she… jealous? It had to be something like that. And it made sense. Clara was beautiful, while Vita was…

Plain?

I'd thought that the first time I'd seen her, but that was before she'd had her hand on my cock; before she'd come so passionately under my hand; before I'd felt the jolt of electricity between us.

No, she wasn't plain. Different, but not plain in the slightest.

'I've changed my mind,' I said, taking her hand in mine and stroking her warm palm. 'I've decided I've got a thing for redheads instead.'

She looked down at where I was holding her hand.

She'd remembered to put the diamond on like a good girl and it sparkled under the lights strung on the trellis above our heads.

'That doesn't mean I'm ready to sleep with you.'

'Who said anything about sleeping?'

'You know what I mean.'

I lifted our linked hands and tugged, pulling her forward against my chest, taking advantage of showing the rest of the bar how in love we were.

Her free hand came out, her palm against my chest, holding herself away. Then she frowned. 'What's that?' She was looking at my throat.

I'd ditched my tie for the evening and the collar of my black business shirt was open, which was normally not an issue. But the way her hand was resting on my chest had pulled the fabric aside, revealing the twisting length of one of my scars.

A jolt of an emotion I couldn't place hit me.

Women had seen my scars before—they were all over my chest and back—but it had never been a big deal. I kept intrusive questions at bay by making sure they were too busy screaming my name to ask about them. And the few that did ask… Well, I always had answers to give them. A car accident. Escape from a burning building. A plane crash.

No one had ever pushed for more.

Apparently, Vita hadn't got the memo.

I wanted to pull the fabric over the scars Thompson had left on my body, wanted to hide them. Strange, when I'd never been ashamed of them before.

Dad had left me to escape Thompson and his men on my own because he wouldn't pay the ransom they'd demanded, and eventually I'd dragged myself back home.

Those scars, though, were a reminder of what I'd made myself into, and I was proud of them. So why I should want to hide them from Vita was anyone's guess.

'It's a scar,' I said levelly, treating it as no big deal.

'I know, but...' She eased the fabric aside a little more. 'It's quite big. Where on earth did you—?'

'Fell off a mountain bike when I was a kid.' I pulled her hand away and brought her palm to my mouth, kissing it. 'You look beautiful, by the way. Did you dress up especially for me? I hope you're not wearing anything underneath that pretty dress.'

Her gaze flickered from my throat to where I held her hand against my mouth, then she met my gaze. 'Doesn't look like a mountain bike scar.'

Curious vixen.

Irritation needled me. I didn't want to go through the tedious business of telling her the truth, or of fielding all the questions she'd have. I didn't want to go through my past at all. That wasn't why we were here.

I opened my mouth and pressed my teeth into the soft flesh of her palm. A sensual warning.

She caught her breath.

'Do we really need to talk about childhood injuries?' I nipped her again. 'I'd much rather take you back to the penthouse and do something much more fun.'

'But I—'

'Did you think about what I did to you in the restaurant? Did you dream about it?' I brushed my mouth over her palm again, feeling the tremble in her arm as

I did so. Suddenly I wanted to know that she'd thought about it. That she'd thought about me.

'Well?' I demanded, getting impatient. 'Did you think about me? Yes or no?'

Something in Vita's gaze sparked.

It made me catch my breath.

'No,' she said.

CHAPTER TWELVE

Vita

It was a lie and I shouldn't have said it, but I wanted to punish him for how badly he was getting under my skin.

Not only had he made me fall apart in that restaurant, but for the last two days I'd been able to think about nothing else. Second-guessing everything that had happened, second-guessing myself.

I didn't want to fall back into the same trap I'd fallen into with Simon. I didn't want to be obsessed or full of doubt.

I didn't want to want him.

Yet I did and it was the strength of it that was getting to me. I hadn't cared about where I was that night at Ocean. I'd let him do whatever he wanted in that hallway, overwhelmed by his intensity and by how much he'd wanted me.

It would be easy to get addicted to that. And if there was one thing I didn't want to ever do again it was to fall for someone who didn't really want me and who'd only hurt me in the end.

Simon had been handsome, like Leon. Charming,

like Leon. He hadn't had Leon's hard edge, but he'd had a touch of badness in him that had made teenage girls' hearts beat faster.

Teenage girls like me.

I'd been in my second to last year of school while he'd been a year ahead, in Clara's year. He'd started paying attention to me for reasons I hadn't known at the time, but which had become clear later on; he'd wanted her and thought being friends with me would get him access to her. I'd stupidly fallen for his charm, not knowing that he was using me, and the night we finally slept together was the night he'd tried and failed to seduce Clara.

He'd taken his disappointment and bitterness out on me and I never knew it until that video had surfaced. Until it had started making the rounds at school and people had started talking and laughing. Humiliating me.

After that, I'd been wary of men, especially handsome men. Luckily, no one had shown interest in me since and I'd been more than okay with that. Until now.

Until Leon.

'No?' he echoed softly, a hard edge running through his voice.

I could barely keep from shivering. 'No,' I repeated, trying to keep the word even. 'I didn't think about you once. I had some results to write up.'

'Liar.' The hard edge was more pronounced now, a smile bordering on savage curving his mouth. 'You thought about me. You thought about my hands on your body and the way I touched you. You thought about how hard you came for me.'

I had. I'd thought about all those things even though

I'd tried not to. They'd made me ache, made me burn, made me want the things I'd told myself I'd never want again: to be desired; to be touched; to feel special; not to feel like an ugly duckling grown up into an ugly duck.

But admitting that felt like giving up some of my power and I didn't want to do that.

My palm pressed against the hard muscle of his chest, trying to get some distance. 'I didn't. Like I said, I was too busy with my test results.'

'Fuck your test results.' His free hand was at the small of my back, not giving me an inch of the distance I wanted. 'No, on second thoughts, fuck me instead.'

My heartbeat thudded even faster, the rough heat in his voice sending chills through me. He was so raw and demanding, leaving me in no doubt about what he wanted.

Me.

Dangerous. You like that too much.

It was and I did, and so I tried to resist.

'That wasn't in the deal,' I said. 'And anyway, I have some—'

Letting out a low growl, Leon shifted the hand holding me in place to the back of my head, fingers curling into my hair. Then he pulled me forward to claim my mouth.

The kiss was scorching and this time there was no subtle invitation to open for him. He simply pushed his tongue deep into my mouth as if he owned it.

The taste of him was devastating and I shuddered as he explored me, achingly conscious of his body resting under mine. I wanted to touch all that heat and hard-packed muscle to see if it felt as perfect as it looked. Yet I also didn't want to give in.

Helpless passion had hurt me before and I was still afraid of it.

I shoved against his chest, panting as he broke the kiss and stared at me.

'What?' His tawny brows pulled down. 'I know you want me, Vita. You can't pretend otherwise, not now.'

I didn't want to admit it but he was right. I opened my mouth to tell him to let me go but, before I could get the words out, he asked suddenly, 'What are you afraid of?'

God, how had he seen my fear? I glanced away, embarrassed.

But he took my chin in his fingers and turned me to face him, his golden eyes unavoidable. 'Is it me?' he asked bluntly.

'No,' I said, my denial instinctive. 'I'm not afraid of you.'

He gave a bitter-sounding laugh. 'Then you're a fool.'

'Why?' This time it was my turn to demand, my attention momentarily diverted. 'Because of your past?'

'We're not talking about me.' His fingers firmed on my chin. 'You're afraid of something and I want to know what it is.'

I didn't want to tell him, didn't want to make myself any more vulnerable than I was already, but the truth came out anyway. 'I'm afraid of…this.' I pushed against his chest for emphasis. 'This…chemistry between us.'

His frown deepened. 'Why? There's nothing wrong with sexual attraction.'

'There is if it's been used against you.'

Realisation dawned in his eyes and my face flamed. I tried to pull away but he only held me tighter.

'Listen to me,' he said, his voice quiet and fierce. 'There are many things you should be afraid of when it comes to me, Vita, but one thing you should never be afraid of is that I'll use your desire to hurt you.' His fingers were firm against my jaw and very warm, his gaze inescapable. 'I'm not so insecure that I need to film a woman and make fun of her in order to feel better about myself. You don't have to believe me, but that's the truth.'

His words dislodged something heavy in my chest, making it shift. 'So why, then?' I asked. 'What is it about me? No one else has ever wanted me. Why should you?'

Golden sparks flickered in his eyes. 'You really want to know?'

I couldn't pretend it wasn't important to me, not now. Not when I'd already given away so much. 'Yes.'

He smiled, an edge of savagery to it. 'I'll show you.'

Before I could respond, he got up off the couch, pulling me with him, and then we were moving to the bar's exit. He'd wound his fingers through mine, tugging me along as we threaded through the tables, and people turned to look at us as we left.

The attention normally would have made me want to run and hide, but tonight all I could think about was where he was leading me and what would happen when we got there. And whether I really wanted to see what it was he was going to show me.

Outside the bar was a long corridor that led to a lift. Leon strode down it then hit the lift button. The doors opened instantly and he pulled me inside. I waited for him to press the ground floor button but, as the doors closed, it was the stop button he pressed instead.

My heart shuddered to a halt then resumed again, harder, faster. Thundering in my head.

The lift was small, the walls mirrored, Leon's tall, broad reflection filling the tiny space.

He turned to me, his hands on my hips, propelling me against the back wall of the lift.

The air around us had got thicker, his amber gaze burning into mine as the tension drew tighter.

I could feel his heat, see the flames of raw desire in his eyes. He wasn't hiding, he wasn't pretending. He was letting me see it—letting me see all of it.

Why did he want me so badly? What was it he saw in me?

My parents had always found me plain and uninteresting. My mother had never understood my lack of interest in clothes and parties; my father had never understood me, full stop. 'Be more like Clara,' he'd advised, and so I'd tried. But I hadn't been any good at that either.

Leon stared down at me, dark and intent, sliding his hands from my hips to my thighs then curling his fingers into the silky fabric of the new green dress a saleswoman had talked me into buying the day before.

'W-what are you going to show me?' I asked shakily, unable to bear the silence.

'You'll see.'

Then he began to ease the hem of my dress up slowly, taking his time, looking down into my face as the fabric rose higher and higher.

I began to tremble, both with inexplicable fear and a deep, thrilling excitement.

'Are you afraid?' he asked softly as the silk brushed over the tops of my thighs, cool air against my skin.

'Yes.' The word came out as a whisper.

One corner of his mouth quirked in a wicked smile. 'It's only chemicals, vixen. Remember?'

My own words come back to haunt me, but he was right.

'Besides,' he went on, easing my dress up to my waist. 'You can stop me whenever you like. But if you do you'll never get to see what I want to show you.'

My throat was dust-dry already, going even drier as his attention dropped from my face down to what he'd uncovered. Me, bare apart from my underwear, from the waist down.

He didn't move. 'Shall I stop?'

I wished I didn't have to make the decision. I wished he could make it for me because if I said yes I'd have no one to blame but myself if it went wrong. But I wasn't sure I could say no.

I ached. I burned. The desire he'd woken in me had been starved for too long and it needed to be fed.

I closed my eyes, shivering.

'Vita.' Impatience threaded his voice. 'Answer me.'

'Don't stop,' I croaked, keeping my eyes shut.

Silence fell.

'Then hold your knickers aside for me, sweetheart,' he murmured at last. 'I want to see that sweet little pussy.'

The blunt eroticism of the words made me blush at the same time as they sent a pulse of raw heat straight through me.

I couldn't do that, could I?

'Look at me,' he ordered.

My eyes flicked open, meeting the burning gold of his, and he leaned forward, resting his forearms on the mirrored surface of the wall on either side of my head, his face inches from mine.

'Do it.' He stared at me, his voice lower, rougher and taut with command. 'Show me what I have to be desperate about.'

The desire in his gaze was so compelling. I couldn't resist him, not any more.

My hands were shaking as I hooked my fingers in the damp fabric of my underwear and pulled it aside, baring myself to him.

He pushed himself away and looked down.

'Fuck.' The word was hoarse, the intentness with which he studied me making my face flame. 'You're a natural redhead. I knew you would be.' He reached out and stroked the curls between my thighs, his fingertips brushing my sensitive flesh. 'I knew you'd be wet too.'

I shuddered, white heat streaking through me at his touch. He glanced up at me again, sliding a finger through my folds in a long, slow stroke that tore a gasp from my throat and sent an intense, brutal kind of pleasure licking up inside me.

His smile was dark as his hands dropped away from my sex, coming to rest on my hips. Then he turned me around so that I faced the back wall of the lift.

The mirrored back wall.

I stared at the woman reflected back at me, her hair all over her shoulders in glossy waves, her face flushed, her mouth full and red. Her eyes were very dark yet they glowed with heat.

A sensual woman. Maybe even a beautiful woman.

Behind her stood a beautiful man, tawny and gold like a lion. All command, all power. A faint line of colour stained his high cheekbones and a muscle leapt in the side of his hard jaw.

He looked like he wanted to eat the woman standing in front of him alive.

'I haven't…d-done this since that video,' I said before I could stop myself, the last gasp of my fear. 'So… p-please go slow.'

His jaw seemed to harden, that muscle at the side of it leaping higher. And all he said was, 'Watch.'

CHAPTER THIRTEEN

Leon

I'D NEVER BEEN so hard in my entire fucking life.

Vita stood in front of me, her wide dark eyes looking at her own reflection in the mirrored wall of the lift then at me standing behind her.

I could see the arousal in her gaze and written all over her face. But there was apprehension there too, and no wonder. If she hadn't had sex since that video then this moment was going to be difficult.

The feelings of others had never bothered me; I simply didn't concern myself with them. But right now, right here, with Vita standing in front of me, I was concerned with her feelings.

She'd been cruelly manipulated and humiliated by some kid who should have known better, and I knew what that felt like. I knew how it messed with your head and how it made you see yourself differently.

Yet it had only been when she'd pushed me away a third time in the bar that I'd truly understood.

I'd automatically thought it had been me that she'd been afraid of, but no, it was the sexual chemistry between us and, though she hadn't said it, I knew it was her own passion too that scared her.

But she didn't need to be afraid. I wouldn't use it to hurt her.

All I wanted to do was use it to give her a different vision of herself. One where she was desired—where she was beautiful, sexy and sensual. Everything that video had told her she wasn't.

I didn't know why it was important she saw that; I just didn't like that she'd been hurt. I didn't like that she'd been made to doubt herself and her desirability either.

I wanted to show her what I'd seen when she'd come apart under my touch at the restaurant.

She trembled as I reached into the back pocket of my trousers for my wallet and extracted the condom inside. I should have said something reassuring, but the scent of her arousal was everywhere and I was on a fucking knife-edge.

I could barely get the condom on, my hands were shaking so badly, let alone speak.

She'd asked me to go slowly but I wasn't going to have a choice. I'd have to go slowly simply to stay in control.

Christ, how had that even happened? How was it that Augustus King's most feared lieutenant was standing in a lift, shaking like a teenage boy seeing a bare pussy for the first time? And all because of one prickly little redhead.

I gripped my cock, staring at her in the reflective surface of the mirror. Correction, one beautiful little redhead.

Auburn hair everywhere, bright eyes, flushed with desire for me.

Couldn't she see what sheer fucking perfection she was?

'Hands on the rail,' I ordered, standing back from her. 'Then bend over. But keep your eyes on the mirror. Don't look away.'

She hesitated only for a moment before grabbing onto the rail that ran around the inside of the lift and bending over, giving me a fantastic view of her perfect ass.

Her dress was up around her waist, revealing the plain dark blue cotton knickers she wore. I wanted them gone, wanted to see more of what she'd shown me earlier, those beautiful reddish curls between her legs. So I hooked my fingers in the waistband and jerked them down her thighs.

She gave a gasp, her gaze meeting mine in the mirror.

I smiled then looked down beyond the white curve of her butt to where soft red curls guarded the slick wet flesh of her pussy.

'Gorgeous,' I said hoarsely, unable to stop looking. 'You're so fucking pretty.' I couldn't resist the urge to touch her, running my fingers over the soft skin of one butt cheek then squeezing it gently. I felt her tremble and when I ran my fingers down further to stroke those silky curls and slick folds, she trembled even harder.

I straightened, dragging my gaze from her pussy to meet her dark eyes in the mirror again. But I kept my fingers between her thighs, finding her hard little clit, circling it. 'Remember to watch. I want you to see how sexy you are.'

She shuddered, her face flushing red as she did as she was told, her knuckles white where she gripped the railing. A soft moan escaped her.

I took my hand away, my fingers covered in her wetness. Making sure she was watching me, I put them in my mouth, licking the salty sweet taste of her from my skin.

Her breath hitched, her expression mesmerised.

'You taste good, sweetheart,' I said. 'So very good. When I get you home I'm going to eat you out, make you scream. But before that happens…'

I moved closer, reaching down with one hand to grip my cock, my other hand on her hip, holding her steady. Then I positioned myself.

'Eyes on your reflection, little vixen.' I rubbed the head of my cock against her slick flesh, teasing her, teasing us both. 'I want you to watch yourself when I push inside you. So you can see what I see.'

She was panting, her breathing loud in the tiny space, and mine wasn't much better, though I was clearly more experienced at controlling it.

I had to do that now as I flexed my hips, pushing against her, easing the head of my dick into her pussy. The feel of her flesh parting around mine, then wet heat surrounding me, gripping me tightly, tore a growl from my throat.

Christ, she was tight. Slick. Hot. So fucking hot.

A long, low groan escaped her as I eased inside. Her gaze was pinned to her reflection, her mouth slightly open, her cheeks deeply flushed, little curls stuck to her forehead like tiny flames.

She looked wanton. Sensual. So desirable it was all I could do not to lose control completely and drive myself inside her until I passed out.

'See?' I gripped her hip, pushing in deeper, as deep as I could get. 'See how beautiful you are. How fucking sexy. And that look in your eyes… Christ, sweetheart. So much passion.' I drew myself out of her in a long, slow glide, pleasure making my fingers dig into the soft flesh of her hip. Then I pushed back in, deeper. Harder. She groaned, gripping tightly to the rail. 'That's what I see, Vita. That's what I want.' I drew back once more before thrusting into her slick heat again, gritting my teeth against the intense rush of pleasure. 'That's what I see in you. That is you.'

She gasped again as I pulled out then made another desperate sound as I thrust back in, her gaze fixed on her reflection in the mirror.

Watching her watch herself as I fucked her, as her pussy gripped me tight as a glove, was the most erotic experience I'd ever had in my life. Because there was wonder in her eyes. As if she was seeing herself for the first time.

I'd done that for her. I'd done that to her.

I'd made her look. I'd made her see how beautiful she was. How passionate.

Me, who'd only ever given others pain.

A hot, possessive feeling uncoiled in my chest, making me growl. Making me slam my cock deeper into her tight sex.

Her gaze came to mine, her eyes black in the dim light, and yet with that paradoxical bright glow. Full of stars.

'Leon.' Her voice was husky and I could hear the desperation in it. 'Oh, God… Leon…'

The way she said my name, as if I was the only one who could give her what she needed, intensified the pleasure that licked up my spine by a million fucking degrees.

I'd wanted to hold her on the edge, fuck her until she was screaming, all the while staying in control myself. But as soon as my name left her mouth I knew that wasn't going to happen.

So I reached around her, slid one hand over her stomach and down, finding her slick little clit. 'Watch,' I said roughly, stroking her as I thrust deep. 'Watch yourself come, sweetheart.'

And she did, her gaze fixed to her own reflection as I slammed deep inside her, holding my finger down and circling, stroking. Then her mouth opened and her back arched and her pussy clamped down hard on my cock as the climax took her. At the last minute, though, it wasn't herself she looked at as she cried out in ecstasy.

It was me.

Staring at me with wonder. With awe. As if I was more than a monster in an expensive suit, a criminal with a pretty face.

As if I was someone worth looking at.

I'd told her what I'd seen in her. But what did she see in me?

Ah, fuck, what did that matter? It didn't. Not when her pussy was rippling around my cock, wet silk and heat and the pleasure that was rapidly making me lose my bloody mind.

All it took was one last thrust and the orgasm took

me like a fucking hammer, exploding in my head. And it wasn't her who ended up screaming and blind with pleasure. It was me, roaring her name, seeing nothing but those bright eyes watching me as I came.

Afterwards I couldn't move—could only stand there with my legs shaking as I tried to get myself the fuck together.

Her head was hanging down, her hands gripping white-knuckled onto the rail, her body trembling as much as mine with the aftershocks.

I pulled out of her slowly, relishing the shiver she gave as I did so, dealing with the condom to dispose of later. Then I turned back to her, pulling her underwear back up and tugging her dress down, smoothing it in place. Slipping an arm around her waist, I got her to straighten then drew her against me, enjoying her soft warmth as she leaned into me, her head tipping back against my shoulder.

She looked at me in the mirror from beneath her lashes, the dark glitter of her eyes making my insatiable cock harden again.

I hadn't thought of what we'd do after I'd been inside her. But now, as I met her gaze, it all became very, very clear.

'I'm taking you home,' I said, not caring how rough my voice sounded. 'To my place. You okay with that?'

She gave a nod.

'And screw whether sex was in our agreement or not,' I went on, because this was not going to be a one-off thing, no way in hell. 'It is now.'

She sighed. 'I suppose there's not much point arguing with you, is there?'

'No.' I spread my hand possessively on her stomach. 'Did you want to?'

'Not really.' She gave me a hesitant look. 'It's just sex, though?'

'Of course.' My gaze sharpened on hers. 'If you're wanting more—'

'I don't.' The words were emphatic. 'Just sex is fine with me. We let the chemical reaction burn itself out, right?'

Ah, yes. She was fond of her chemicals, wasn't she?

'Right,' I confirmed. Satisfaction spread through me, and I turned my head into her neck, nipping at her delicate skin possessively.

In the mirror her mouth curved. She had a lovely smile and the knowledge that I'd put it there made my heart beat hard.

'I owe you a thank you,' she said quietly.

'For what?'

'For showing me what you did. For making me see myself.'

The stark honesty in the words reached inside me, making my chest feel tight and uncomfortable.

Most people ended up cursing my name rather than thanking me and I'd never got any gratitude from my father for all the years of service I'd given him.

'Anyone could have done that for you, sweetheart,' I said, making light of it, because Christ knew I didn't want heavy. 'All you needed was some appreciation. Lots of guys can give you that.'

'Lots of guys might but you were the one who noticed and saw what I needed in the first place.' Her expression was serious, her gaze searching mine. 'And you were the one who cared enough to give it to me.'

That honesty again—fuck, it was a killer. Some part of me loved it, lapping that up and her gratitude along with it like a thirsty dog with a bowl of water. Yet at the same time another part of me hated it.

She shouldn't be grateful to a man who'd once used violence and blackmail the same way a builder used a hammer and nails. Not when she'd already been targeted by one bastard, and certainly not when I was an even bigger bastard than the man who'd filmed her.

I might have left my days of violence and blackmail behind me, but that didn't mean I was a good man.

'Why did you do that?' she asked when I didn't speak.

'You ask too many questions, sweetheart,' I murmured and, bending my head, I kissed her hard.

Before she could ask me anything else that I didn't have the answer to.

CHAPTER FOURTEEN

Vita

I WOKE UP SUDDENLY, not sure what had woken me. It might have been because I wasn't in my own bed in my little terrace house in Newtown, but in Leon's penthouse apartment overlooking Sydney Harbour.

The walls of the bedroom were nothing but windows and he didn't like obscuring the incredible view with something as mundane as blinds. Which meant I'd been woken at sunrise each morning after our last couple of dates with dawn flooding into the room and Leon's hands on my body, working his magic with his mouth and his fingers. And his cock.

But it wasn't dawn now and the bed beside me was empty.

In fact, it was full night, the lights of the harbour stretched out in front of me, with the Opera House below and beyond that the bridge in a shining arc.

No point in trying to go back to sleep. I probably wouldn't, not when Leon wasn't there.

I slipped out of bed, searching around for my clothes before remembering they were out in the lounge, where Leon had ripped them off me after we'd got back from the nightclub.

Our fourth date and we hadn't even been there half an hour before Leon leaned in and whispered in my ear that the club could go fuck itself. He wanted to fuck me instead.

That had been the pattern after he'd taken me in the lift. We'd meet up in public, make a desultory attempt at conversation, then go back to his place where he'd have me naked and screaming his name within minutes.

Perhaps I should have been worried that every time he touched me I'd become putty in his hands. But I told myself that was simply due to the physical chemistry that we were burning out, and once that was gone it would be over.

Besides, in the mirrors of the lift that night, he'd shown me something in myself that I'd never seen before, a beauty and sensuality that I'd always thought was my sister's, never mine. But I'd seen it as he pushed into me and the pleasure had taken hold—as I watched myself come apart in the mirror right in front of me.

It should have been exposing but it wasn't.

With him behind me, the evidence of his desperation driving into me, his dark amber gaze pinned to our reflections, I'd felt beautiful for the first time in my life. Desirable. Wanted.

All the things I'd wanted to feel with Simon and hadn't.

It was the first time I'd ever felt any of those things and I couldn't give them up, not yet. Not while Leon could give them to me.

Anyway, I'd be careful to make sure only my body surrendered. Everything else remained my own and that was how it would stay.

Since my clothes weren't there, I found the dark blue shirt Leon had been wearing earlier that evening discarded over a low white chair opposite the bed and put it on.

I shivered as his warm scent enveloped me, making hunger turn over in my gut. I wanted him again, craved his touch and the way he made me feel.

He'd told me anyone could give me that, but he was wrong. No one had bothered looking past my façade for years, because no one had been interested enough.

But he had.

He hadn't given me an answer as to why, or what he got out of sleeping with me, not when there were plenty of women far more beautiful than I was to choose from, but unusually for me, I'd decided not to question further. Some things didn't stand up to scientific testing; you simply had to accept them for what they were. And I was sure that the sexual relationship I had with Leon wouldn't stand up to any kind of testing at all.

The thought made me uneasy. I wasn't used to not questioning things I didn't understand, but I didn't want anything to disturb the delicate balance between Leon and me so I ignored the feeling.

Moving out of the bedroom, I went down the long hallway that led to the lounge area.

It was a beautiful space, lots of windows to let in the brilliant sun and the amazing view. The walls were as pale as the carpet, the furniture upholstered in the same shades. It was clean, minimalist and very, very sophisticated.

I paused in the doorway, finding Leon sitting on the low white sofa, bare feet propped on the coffee table in front of him, laptop in his lap, staring down at it. He wore only his suit trousers, the light from the screen illuminating the cut muscles of his chest and abs and throwing shadows off his strong jaw and high cheekbones.

My heart squeezed at the sheer masculine beauty of him.

It seemed incredible that someone so breathtakingly beautiful should be mine. Or at least mine for a little while. And that he should find me just as beautiful and desirable as I found him.

Sometimes it felt like a dream. The secret fantasy of the 'I Love You Girl'. Where the ugly duckling didn't have to be a swan at all; she could be just a duck and be wanted all the same.

I leaned my head against the doorframe, staring at him, breathless. My fingers itched, longing to explore that hard-muscled body. Yet the nights we'd been together he'd strip me naked and spread me out on the floor of the lounge, or the couch or up against the window, and explore me with abandon, all the lights on so he could see me.

But when it came to me touching him, he'd be reticent. Not letting me until we were in the bedroom and the lights were off. It was another thing I hadn't questioned since he was good at distracting me. However, I was thinking about it now and it puzzled me.

Getting to know him hadn't seemed important before, not when our marriage wouldn't be a real one, yet it suddenly felt important to me now.

He'd shown me why he wanted me, healing a wound I hadn't known was still painful, yet what did he get out of sleeping with me? Physical pleasure, sure, but there had to be something else. Something he couldn't get from those other, more beautiful women.

I took the opportunity to study him while he wasn't aware of me, the scientist in me now firmly in control.

Faint lines tracked the golden skin of his torso, criss-crossing his abs and then, further up, his chest. Some of them were long and twisted, others merely small hollows. They were difficult to see in the pale light of the computer, but I knew what they were. Scars. Old ones.

I frowned. I'd felt them when I'd touched him in the darkness and in the rooftop bar that night I'd caught a glimpse of the one at his throat. He'd told me he'd got it from a mountain bike accident. But they didn't look like the kinds of scars you got in an accident.

Don't forget who he is.

A kernel of ice gathered in my gut. I had forgotten. He was the son of Augustus King, once Sydney's biggest crime boss. And not only that. Leon had been his lieutenant. I didn't know exactly what that meant, but he'd probably done some bad stuff and maybe those scars were evidence of that.

I shivered as reality crept into the bubble of happy sexual pleasure I'd surrounded myself with.

How could I have forgotten that there was always going to be more to him than the handsome, charming stranger who'd seduced me? That, although he might have made me feel good about myself, he'd done other things. Things that did not involve making people feel good about themselves.

You can't keep yourself in the dark. Not this time.

No, I couldn't. I was going to have to ask the hard questions. But at least with Leon, if I didn't like the answers I wouldn't lose anything.

'Miss me?' Leon said unexpectedly, not looking up from his screen.

'Yes.' Trying not to show my surprise that he'd spotted me, I pushed myself away from the doorway, forcing myself over to where he sat on the couch. Fear crept through me and I didn't know why. Was it him I was afraid of? Or was it what I might find out about him? Or was it simply that this affair might end and I didn't want it to? 'I woke up and you weren't there.'

'Just keeping track of what the media are saying about us.' His long fingers moved quickly over the touchpad, opening up the browser tab instead.

His hands weren't scarred, I couldn't help noting. Just his torso.

'What are they saying?' Not that I was interested. I was more interested in the pattern of small round scars at the top of his six-pack instead. They looked like…cigarette burns.

'Mostly that it's a shocking scandal.' The wicked smile I'd come to know so well over the past few days curled his mouth. 'And they love it. Quite a few are on your side, believe it or not. They love the fact that the "I Love You Girl" has managed to snag Mr Tall, Blond and Dangerous. And that's a direct quote.'

Talk of the media momentarily distracted me from his scars. I'd had a few calls from various news outlets, wanting interviews and the inside story on how Leon and I had got together, as well as what I'd been doing for the past ten years since my video had gone viral.

I'd ignored them. Not because I was ashamed this time, but because I simply didn't care what the media said. I was too busy glorying in the pleasure he gave me every night to worry about it.

'Tall, blond and dangerous?' I echoed.

'Hey, is it my fault they find me irresistible?' He reached out and toyed with the hem of the shirt I wore, which ended mid-thigh. 'But what I really like is this. You wearing anything under that? No, wait, don't tell me. I want to find out for myself.' His tawny brows drew together all of a sudden, his dark amber gaze zeroing in on me in a way that made me uneasy. 'What's wrong?'

That stare pinned me, making my breath catch.

Did I really want to broach this topic? Did I really want to test what was happening between us by asking him about his past?

You know the answer to that.

Of course. I was a scientist. And I needed answers.

I glanced down at the pattern of scars on his stomach and the ones slashing across his chest. I brushed my fingers over the small round scars that peppered his abs. 'You never did say where you got these.'

Leon closed the laptop with a snap, the light from the screen cutting off and plunging the room back into darkness. Then he grabbed my hand from his skin and moved it down to where I could feel him rapidly hardening under the fabric of his trousers.

'Yes, I did. But I think you should wonder about how you could fix this instead.' He flexed his hips in blatant invitation. 'I guarantee it'll be a lot more interesting.'

His face was shadowed in the dim light from the city outside the windows, his expression hidden. But I knew a distraction technique when I saw one.

He hadn't wanted to talk about those scars that night in the bar, and it seemed he didn't want to talk about them now either.

Are you sure you want to keep going?

No, I wasn't sure. But if we were going to continue to sleep together I needed to know just how dangerous this man truly was. Not that I was worried about my physical safety—I was sure he'd never hurt me. It was my peace of mind I was worried about.

'You said a mountain bike accident.' I shook his hand off and reached out to touch him again. 'But these look like—'

His fingers closed around my wrist and it wasn't a playful hold this time. It was hard, his fingertips digging into my skin. 'They're not for you.' His voice had turned flat. 'If you want to touch me, put your hand on my cock instead.'

Okay, he definitely didn't want to talk about them. And maybe it wasn't any wonder since they must have been painful. But those round ones… Had someone ground out a cigarette on his skin?

The chill inside me deepened, horror rising as I stared at the scars. He'd been hurt. No, more than merely hurt. It looked like he'd been…

Tortured.

'No.' A low growl of warning cut into my thoughts. 'This is what you should be paying attention to.' And he shoved my palm insistently to the hard ridge beneath his fly.

But I couldn't drag my gaze from those scars—a stark reminder of who he was. What he was…

'I thought you weren't afraid of me.'

The sharp note in his voice made me look up and meet the laser-like intensity of his gaze. 'I—'

'But you are. I can see it in your eyes. Why? You weren't before.' His grip on my wrist tightened, though I'm sure he wasn't aware of it, not when he was too busy staring at me. 'What did I do?'

There wasn't any point denying my unease, not when he'd picked up on it. 'Nothing,' I said, being honest because he hadn't done anything. 'It's just… those scars, Leon. They reminded me that I don't know anything about you. About your past…' I stopped, my throat dry. 'I think I need to know. Before this goes any further.'

'This?' The question sounded neutral but the grip on my wrist was not.

I gathered my courage. 'This being us, sleeping together.'

'I thought it was only sex. That's what you said.'

'I know. But—'

'But you don't want to sleep with a killer.'

The words were harsh, his voice harsher, but all I had to give him was honesty. 'No,' I said. 'I don't.

His grip loosened and he released me. 'So principled. I admire that, Vita.' Letting out a breath, he leaned back against the couch. 'Even if it pisses me off.'

'Leon, I—'

'I'm not a killer,' he interrupted flatly. 'Dad had

other people who did that for him. But I did hurt people on Dad's orders. I punished them, made them see things his way.'

Was it relief I felt? I wasn't sure.

'Do you still do that? For your brothers?'

'No. That would make us criminals and we're not criminals.' He laughed without amusement. 'At least, not any more.'

Yet not exactly blameless either.

I should have left it then, taken those answers at face value and been satisfied. But it wasn't enough. I had questions and the scientist in me couldn't leave them alone.

'And those scars?' I asked. 'Did you get those making people "see things his way"?'

'Why do you want to know? What difference does it make?'

'Why don't you want to tell me?'

'Because those scars mean nothing.' His eyes gleamed in the darkness. 'Maybe I simply got what I deserved.'

Bitterness laced the words and I studied him, trying to figure out why. 'Those scars look like you were… tortured.'

He lifted a shoulder as if bored of the conversation. 'Like I said, they mean nothing.'

But they did and I knew it. That bitterness gave it away.

'You can tell me,' I said before I could stop myself, wanting to give him something. 'You can tell me anything. I won't judge you. You can trust me.'

His whole body tensed, tight as a coiled spring, and danger thickened in the atmosphere around us. I couldn't tell his expression in the dim light, but there was no mistaking the menace glowing in his eyes.

He did not want to talk about this.

You need to stop pushing.

My pulse had sped up, my breath coming faster. Yes, I should, but he'd been hurt and I wanted to know why. He knew about my scars, the ones that weren't physical but were there all the same, the ones that had been inflicted by Simon and that video. He knew and had helped them hurt a little bit less, so why couldn't I do the same for him? At least I could try.

'Why should I trust you?' His tone was silky with menace. 'You're only the woman I'm sleeping with at the moment. Nothing else.'

An inexplicable hurt slid under my skin, though there was no reason it should. I was only the woman he was sleeping with and I didn't want to be anything more. Did I?

Yet...he sounded so bitter. Did he have anyone in his life he could trust? There were his brothers and I didn't know what kind of relationships he had with them, but he must trust them. He didn't need me poking at things that weren't my business.

'What?' he demanded. 'You want to say something?'

'Is there anyone you do trust?' The question was out before I could think better of it.

Instantly, his expression became shuttered and that was when I knew.

No. He didn't.

Determination shifted and turned inside me. When my video had hit, when everyone I'd trusted had betrayed me, the only person I'd had was my aunt. She hadn't been a warm person but she'd taught me to bake, and it had been in the moments when we were in the kitchen, just the two of us, measuring and weighing the ingredients, that I'd talked to her about my experience. She'd never said much in response, but she didn't judge, didn't blame. Simply let me talk.

Did Leon need someone to talk to? Did he have anyone he could talk to?

It hit me then—the reasons I was asking myself all these questions. I wanted him to talk to me. I wanted him to trust me.

But simply telling him he should wasn't going to work, and why should it? Given his past, he wouldn't be a man who trusted easily.

Which meant that if I wanted this I had to give him a reason.

I went with my instinct. Bending to pick up his laptop, I opened up the video programme that operated the camera. Then I put the computer down on the coffee table, angling it so the camera was directed at him and his whole body was in the shot.

Ignoring the frantic beat of my heart, I hit Record then turned back, moving to straddle his legs where they rested on the table in front of him.

A ripple of emotion crossed his face. He glanced at the computer, where the pair of us were on the screen, then back at me, surprised.

'What are you doing?'

I lifted my hands to the buttons of the shirt and slowly began to undo them. 'Giving you a reason to trust me.'

He glanced at the computer again and I saw realisation hit. Abruptly, he tried to grab my wrists. 'You don't need to—'

I shook his fingers off, letting the shirt slip from my shoulders.

A week ago, baring my body for a man like this, let alone to yet another camera, would have filled me with dread. But I couldn't think of any other way to show him how serious I was. If I wanted his trust, I had to show him he had mine.

'Don't turn it off,' I said fiercely. 'I want it to record us. I want to give you something I wouldn't ever give anyone else. Because I trust you.'

Shock left his face momentarily blank and a small spark of triumph went through me, pleased that I'd surprised him so completely. But I didn't let myself dwell on it. Instead, I took his hands and guided them to my breasts, shivering at the contact of his warm skin on mine.

'Why?' His voice was hoarse and he stared at me like I was a stranger. 'I haven't done a single fucking thing to deserve this.'

'You have.' I pressed his palms against my flesh, letting him feel how my nipples hardened in response. 'You made me feel beautiful. You made me feel wanted. You made me feel special.'

'Vita—'

'You need someone to talk to, Leon. You need someone to trust. And you can trust me.' Then I leaned forward, crushing his hands between our bodies as I brushed my mouth over his.

He was still for a second. Then he jerked his hands from between us, the fingers of one hand burying themselves in my hair while he wound his arm around my waist, pulling me tight against him.

And he took control of the kiss.

His tongue swept into my mouth, the heat and taste of him flooding my senses, so demanding that my fingers curled into his chest, trying to hold on to something—anything.

He was hard and hot beneath me, the wool of his suit trousers rubbing against the sensitive flesh of my bare sex and inner thighs. The feel of his chest against my nipples, smooth skin, firm muscle and the slight prickle of hair, was glorious.

I dug my nails into him, kissing him as desperately as he was kissing me, shivering as his teeth closed on my bottom lip in a short, hard nip.

Then I found myself flipped over onto my back on the couch, with him lying half on his side, half over me, golden eyes hot and possessive as he looked down at me.

'I'll tell you where my scars came from,' he said. 'On one condition. I want something pretty to look at and beautiful to touch when I do.'

I didn't understand what he meant at first. Then he cupped my breast in one large, warm palm and dragged his thumb with aching slowness over my nipple, making me gasp.

Pretty to look at and beautiful to touch...

He was talking about me.

My chest tightened and my eyes prickled. A ridiculously emotional reaction that I was powerless to stop. So, not only had he accepted my offer of trust, he was still making me feel beautiful with it.

I didn't know what I'd done to deserve it but this

time I stayed quiet, not risking speaking in case he changed his mind.

'When I was fifteen,' Leon began, 'I was taken by some enemies of my father. They targeted me because my older brother Ajax was too dangerous and my younger brother was too well protected. But I wasn't. I was the middle child and pretty, a bookworm, easy prey.' He looked down to his hand on my breast, watching his thumb circle my nipple once more. 'They held me for a couple of days, trying to get money out of my father, but he wouldn't pay the ransom.'

His touch sent a lightning strike of pleasure from my breast straight to my sex, but through it I felt a deep foreboding settling down in my bones.

'They were…unhappy with my father's response,' he went on, his voice expressionless, his nail scraping gently against my sensitive nipple, making me tremble. 'So they took it out on me. With knives, cigarettes. One of them had a baseball bat and I got a few broken ribs from that.'

Despite the heat of pleasure, I felt cold. Oh, God, they had tortured him.

'Leon…' I began.

But he shook his head. 'No. Stay quiet.' His nail scraped over me again, making the pulse of pleasure between my thighs more intense. 'They would have killed me if I hadn't escaped. But I did.' His hand slid from my breast down my body, his gaze following it as his fingers grazed the curls between my thighs. 'They thought I was asleep, but I wasn't. I got out, got myself back home and demanded Dad tell me why he hadn't rescued me; why he wouldn't pay the ransom.' His fingers delicately parted my sensitive flesh and I couldn't stop the moan that escaped me as he found my clit, circling it gently. 'Do you know why he wouldn't? Because I was expendable. Because Ajax was the oldest and Xander was the clever one. But I was the pretty one, the useless one. I wasn't worth the time it would have taken for a rescue or the money for the ransom.'

He wasn't looking at me, watching his finger stroking my sex instead, which somehow made it that much hotter. So much so that it was difficult to focus on what he was saying and not get lost in the tide of pleasure slowly rising inside me. 'Dad only surrounded himself with people who were useful to him and apparently being his son wasn't enough. So I decided to make myself useful. I became his weapon, dangerous enough that no one would ever target me again.' He glanced at me at the same time as he eased one finger into me, going slow and deep, tearing a moan from my throat. His eyes were molten, glittering. 'And no one did, Vita. You know why? Because I made sure they were all too afraid of me.'

The pleasure was intense and I could barely hear him over the frantic beat of my heart and the overwhelming urge to lift my hips, ride that finger. But the hard note in his voice and the anger in his eyes stopped me from losing myself entirely.

So, he'd been tortured because his father hadn't thought he was worth rescuing. At fifteen.

Behind my ribs, my heart clenched tight.

That was so wrong. So awful. It had upset me that, after my video had hit, all my own father had thought about was the effect it was having on his business and the family's reputation rather than me. But at least he hadn't left me in the hands of people who'd hurt me, who'd possibly even kill me, just because I wasn't useful to him.

'Leon, stop.' I reached to pull his hand away because it felt wrong to be receiving such pleasure while he relived something so awful.

But he simply held my wrist down by my side and slid another finger into me, stretching me. 'I told you,' he said, rough and fierce. 'I want something beautiful to touch.'

I panted, unable to stop my back from arching or from lifting my hips in time with the movements of his fingers. 'But… I… I can't feel this while you… talk about t-torture.'

'Yes, you can. I'd rather you felt pleasure than pain. Or anything else for that matter.' He bent his head, his tongue finding my nipple and circling it as his fingers slid deep inside me. I groaned, the feel of his mouth incandescent. 'So don't feel sorry for me, vixen,' he murmured against my skin. 'Just scream my name when you come.'

But I didn't feel sorry for him. I felt nothing but a terrible sympathy while at the same time I was furious at the people who'd done this to him. His father, who hadn't even bothered looking for him, let alone rescuing him. While he'd had knives, cigarettes pressed against his skin, a baseball bat…

'Leon,' I whispered. 'You shouldn't…'

'Give me this, Vita.' A raw note had entered his voice. 'This is what I want to think about. The way you feel and the way you taste. Give me your pleasure. Give me something good that I can do for you. Please.'

He'd never said that word to me before. He'd never begged. And I couldn't deny him. I didn't have any advice or any words of wisdom. Nothing else to give him, apart from myself. My trust and my body.

So I gave him both.

'Okay,' I murmured.

He shifted, gripping my thigh and pushing it out, pressing it against the back of the couch, holding me open as he stared down at my exposed sex. Then he touched me with his free hand, stroking me, spreading my wet flesh, burying the terrible thing he'd told me under the delicate stroke of pleasure.

Holding me open, he bent his head and covered my sex with his mouth. I jerked in his grip, the slide of his tongue against my clit electric, lighting up every nerve ending I had.

I groaned, arching up into him as he licked and explored my slick flesh, as the hand on my thigh firmed, keeping me spread so he could sink his tongue deep inside me.

'Leon!' My hands groped for him, finding the softness of his hair. I wound my fingers in the thick silk of it, holding on tight as he brought his free hand into play, touching and stroking me as he licked me.

'Yes,' he murmured against me, his voice thick with satisfaction. 'Tell me who's making you come. Tell me who's making you scream. Say my name, vixen.'

And I did, helplessly screaming it again as he pushed me off the edge of the world.

CHAPTER FIFTEEN

Leon

SHE WAS LAID out beneath me, naked and trembling, the sound of my name echoing in the room around us. Her eyes were fixed to mine, sweat beading her forehead and gathering in the hollow of her throat.

I was so hard I ached.

The salty sweet taste of her was in my mouth and I wanted to stay with my head buried between her legs, eating her out all night.

Forgetting everything I'd told her. Forgetting all about that fucking bastard Thompson and what he and his henchmen had done to me.

Forgetting about the note of desperation in my voice, the raw sound of pain. Of weakness.

I thought I'd put those memories behind me, thought they didn't matter any more, but telling her about Thompson had brought them all flooding back in vivid fucking Technicolor.

But I wasn't that sobbing, pathetic fifteen-year-old any more. I was someone much deadlier. Ajax had helped me craft myself into a weapon and, even though I no longer used violence, I was still lethal.

I was still fucking dangerous.

Fury burned in my veins and I wanted to punish her for making me tell her about my scars. For the mistake of giving me her trust.

I wanted to remind her who she was dealing with.

The angle of the laptop wouldn't have captured her face as I'd eaten her out, but I knew what to do so it would.

I leaned down and gathered her up in my arms, bringing her into my lap so she was facing me, straddling my thighs. She was panting, the heat of her pussy soaking through the wool of my trousers, making my cock ache. It would be so easy to unzip myself, slide into her welcoming heat, but that camera would only capture her back and I didn't want that.

I looked into her eyes, glazed and black with pleasure. 'Time to return the favour, sweetheart. Get on your knees.'

I should have known that Vita wouldn't do the expected thing and she didn't now. Instead of instantly obeying, she leaned forward and kissed me, her mouth hot and demanding, her tongue seeking, as if she wanted to taste herself on me.

I lifted my hand to her hair, intending to drag her mouth away and push her down to kneel in front of me, but I couldn't. Her kiss was such a sweet mix of inexperience and demand that I wound my fingers into her hair and held her there instead.

The lick of her tongue, the scrape of her teeth over my lip was electric, the taste of her like honey. I was desperate to devour her but the hungry way she kissed me did things to me, sucking away all my anger and giving me desire in its place.

She left me breathless.

Then suddenly her mouth was gone, trailing down over my jaw and my neck, her lips pressing against my throat. Going further, her tongue licking along the line of the scar Thompson's knife had left on me.

I didn't know why that made me feel like my heart was slowly being squeezed in a giant fist. And when her mouth moved down, tracing the line of each and every scar, the cigarettes they'd ground out on my chest and stomach, the twisted line where the baseball bat had broken the skin, that fist squeezed tighter.

Making me weak. Leaving me vulnerable.

'Vita.' I gripped her hair, tugging her head away. 'No.'

But her black eyes were bright with determination. 'I want to give you better memories,' she said huskily. 'Let me, the way I let you.'

But I already had the taste and feel of her beautiful body, the sound of her screaming my name instead of the pain of the knife and the burn of the cigarettes. The scent of her arousal instead of the smell of my own flesh burning.

I didn't need her delicate tongue and her mouth tracing the reminders of how weak I'd been.

I gripped her hair tighter. 'No.'

'Please,' she said. 'You know you can trust me.'

Trust, fuck. I had no idea what that meant any more, if I ever had. Or why she offered it to me without guile or manipulation, her honesty laid bare in her eyes.

Such a mistake. She needed to protect herself better, especially from men like me.

I opened my mouth to tell her no, but she leaned forward again, giving me another of those sweet, soul-stealing kisses, and somehow I couldn't bring myself to pull her away again.

So I sat there, my fingers wound in the silkiness of her hair, letting her kiss her way down my body. Letting her lick and taste each mark, each scar. Tracing them then putting her mouth over them like she was sucking poison from a snakebite.

Thompson's knife had undone me with pain and now Vita was undoing me with pleasure. I should stop her, take control of the situation again, show her that she couldn't mess with me the way she was doing, but…

Christ. My pulse thundered in my head, my cock aching like a bastard, and I couldn't drag my gaze away from that little pink tongue, watching it on my skin as she went lower and lower.

And it struck me that I'd never been touched like this before. Oh, women had gone down on me—I liked a blow job; what man didn't? But I'd never let anyone run their tongue over my scars or trace them with their fingers. I'd never told anyone what they were or what they meant.

I'd never told anyone about them, full stop.

Yet I'd not only told Vita, I'd let her touch me too.

Vita, with her bright black eyes and her honesty, her trust and her passion.

Slipping between my thighs to kneel on the floor, she then reached to unzip me. I hadn't bothered with underwear when I'd got up earlier so there was nothing between her cool fingers and my rock-hard cock as she opened my trousers and drew me out.

My breath escaped in a hiss as she wrapped those fingers around me, her hair trailing silkily over my thighs and stomach as she bent forward. Then her lips brushed the head of my dick and a growl escaped my throat.

I reached down, gathering her hair in my fist and away from her face so I could watch that pretty tongue lick me.

'More,' I demanded, unable to help myself.

But she ignored me, licking, nipping, making me jerk and shiver under her touch, making me growl yet again.

I'd taught her what I liked in a blow job over the course of the past few days, and I liked it rough, with teeth and a firm touch. But she wasn't doing that now. She was being careful, delicate. Teasing me with gentleness. I wanted to push her head down on me, make her take me all the way to the back of her throat, yet…

I liked this. I liked the care she was taking with me and I had no bloody idea why.

Her tongue swirled, and I gritted my teeth, holding on to her hair as another electric jolt of pleasure hit. 'Put me in your mouth,' I ordered, though it sounded more like a plea. 'Fuck, Vita. Do it.'

Those perfect red lips closed around my cock and she watched me all the while, the heat of her mouth making me lose what little breath I had left.

'Jesus,' I forced out as her fingers tightened around my dick. 'Vixen…'

Then she sucked me. Slow and deep, fast and shallow. Hard then soft. Letting me see my own hard flesh disappearing into her mouth then sliding back out again.

I couldn't take my eyes off her.

The whole world shrank down to this moment. I

forgot about Thompson and his fucking knives. I forgot about the scars marking me and how she'd undone me with her kisses. Forgot about the camera on the laptop recording us. I forgot about everything except her midnight gaze and the stars glittering in it. And her mouth surrounding me, taking me in so deep I could finally feel the back of her throat, her fingers squeezing me tight, pumping me.

I lifted my hips in time with the suction, the pleasure winding tighter and tighter, a hot ball of it at the base of my spine, ready to explode.

Then she lifted her lips a moment and whispered, 'Say my name,' before swallowing me down again, her fingers tight around my dick. She made a soft, satisfied sound that vibrated against my aching flesh and, just like that, the hot ball of pleasure detonated, a column of fire shooting straight up my spine, exploding like a bomb in my head.

My fingers tightened in her hair and I thrust helplessly up into her mouth, roaring her name as I came.

Afterwards, my ears ringing, my body pulsing with the aftershocks, I hauled her up off the floor, putting her onto her back on the couch then shifting over her.

She put her arms around my neck, giving a delicious little shiver as I settled between her thighs. My cock brushed the wet folds of her pussy, already getting hard at the contact, but she gave no sign of noticing, her dark eyes serious as they searched my face.

'Leon, I—' she began.

But I'd said all I wanted to say about it for the night so I laid a finger over her mouth. 'No more,' I murmured. 'I gave you what you wanted. That's enough.'

Frustration flickered in her expression. 'But I want

to talk about you. Why don't you tell me what you were like as a child?'

She was very warm under me and the smell of sex and feminine musk was heady. I could suddenly think of a million things I wanted to do more than talk about my childhood, and all of them included her naked body.

'Why?' I flexed my hips so my cock slid against her slick flesh. 'I'd rather fuck you senseless.'

She hissed, catching her bottom lip between her teeth. I wanted to bite it myself so I leaned down, but she jerked her head to the side, avoiding me. 'No, not yet.'

I growled, but she refused to be distracted. 'Come on, Leon. I'm curious.'

So she didn't want to play.

I debated trying to convince her, but then dismissed the idea. Clearly, she wasn't going to give up until I'd given her what she wanted. Bloody determined little vixen.

'What was I like as a kid?' I said, surrendering. 'I was quiet. I liked to read a lot. When I was about ten I got heavily into computers and computer games.'

Amusement glittered in her eyes. 'So, nerdy then?'

I thought about my younger self. Trying to escape the reality of his life any way he could, with books at first then in the glow of the computer screen and the roar of computer-generated gunfire.

'You could say that,' I agreed.

Amusement turned to mischief. 'Computer club at school?'

'Naturally. All the best people were in the computer club at school.'

'I know.' She grinned. 'I was in the computer club. And the science club. And the photography club. In fact, if there was a club you can pretty much guarantee that I was part of it.'

Curious, I searched for the teenager she'd once been in the sharp, lovely face of the controlled adult she'd become. She would have been bright. Intense. Passionate.

If I'd met her in high school I would have thought she was amazing, I realised. My childhood had been overshadowed by the reality of my father's business and his ruthlessness when it came to running it; Vita's intensity would have been a bright light shining in the darkness…

Christ, I wouldn't only have thought she was amazing. I would have fallen head over heels for her.

'I wish I'd known you then,' I said before I could stop myself. 'I think I would have liked you.'

Her smile became radiant. As if I'd given her a gift. 'I think I would have liked you too. Though you'd probably have intimidated the hell out of me.'

'Oh, really?'

She blushed. 'You're hot—and hot boys were always intimidating.'

'Why?'

'Only a very hot person would ask that question.'

Ah.

I flexed my hips again, loving the feel of her against me. 'You shouldn't have been intimidated. Don't you know you're beautiful?'

She caught her breath but that smile still tugged at her mouth. 'That sounds like a song lyric.'

'All my best pick-up lines are song lyrics.' I stared

down at her. 'Seriously, though, I mean it. You're lovely. I thought I showed you that in the mirror in the lift.'

'You did. But it's hard to accept sometimes, especially when it's always been made clear to you that you're not.'

I frowned, stroking the hair back from her forehead. 'That bastard Simon has a lot to answer for.'

'Not only Simon. My parents aren't exactly supportive types. Clara was the one with the looks in my family, which was pointed out to me a lot.'

Her insecurities made sense to me all of a sudden. A beautiful sister and parents who couldn't see what I saw—the passion, the honesty, the bright-eyed curiosity...

'Poor Clara,' I said. 'She only got looks. You got brains and beauty.'

Vita flushed. 'I wasn't fishing, if that's what you think.'

'I know you're not. I'm just giving you the truth.' And I let her see it in my gaze. 'Brains. Beauty. Honesty. Passion. You got it all, vixen.'

Her mouth curved, pleasure alight in her eyes. Then it faded, her expression turning serious. 'You're very good for me, Leon King. But you're also very bad. You probably need to stop.'

I didn't know what she meant by that.

Are you sure you don't?

Okay, maybe I did. And maybe I liked it. Especially the being good for her part.

I liked that very much.

'Do you really want me to stop?' I ran my hands down her sides then slid my palms beneath the curve of her butt. Gathering her flesh in my palms, I squeezed her lightly. 'Because I'm okay with being good for you.'

Her breath caught. 'Maybe…you don't need to stop that part.'

'What about the bad?' I slipped my fingers between her thighs, searching, exploring. 'I definitely don't want to be bad for you.'

She gave a soft gasp as my fingers found soft, wet flesh, then groaned. 'I think you should stop talking.'

I grinned. And stopped talking.

CHAPTER SIXTEEN

Vita

ALL THAT SEX should have knocked me out cold but I couldn't sleep. My head was too full of the terrible things Leon had told me and his understandable reluctance to talk about them.

Eventually, after tossing and turning, I slipped off the couch, leaving Leon fast asleep beside me, picking up his shirt again and putting it on. Then I got the throw that had been hung over the arm of the couch and covered him with it, being sure not to wake him.

As I drew the throw up around his bare shoulders I looked down at him, my heart aching.

His father must have been one hell of a bastard to have left him in the hands of the monsters who'd hurt him. No wonder he'd set about making himself dangerous. No wonder he'd turned himself into a weapon.

He'd done everything he could to protect himself.

Unsettled, I turned from him and, after a second's thought, went into the pristine minimalist stainless steel and white tile kitchen.

I loved kitchens. They were my laboratory for the wonderful chemistry that was baking, and Leon's kitchen was up there with the best. I wandered around it, checking out cupboards and poking my nose in drawers, opening up the oven to have a look.

Then, needing something to distract myself, I went over to the pantry to see what kind of baking ingredients he had. Not many, but the basics were there.

In the early days after I'd been sent to live with my aunt, when I couldn't sleep I would sometimes get up in the middle of the night and bake something. The focus it required had given me a break from my thoughts, plus I loved that it was chemistry without having to be in a lab.

I didn't think Leon would mind if I used his kitchen, so I set about whipping up a quick batch of scones. I'd been experimenting with an old recipe my aunt had given me, trying to get the best rise, but I hadn't had much luck. So now I pushed all thoughts of Leon's past out of my mind as I bustled about, getting the ingredients out.

Totally absorbed, I made two batches and was just getting the second batch out of the oven when a deep, husky male voice said from behind me, 'Do I want to know why you're baking scones in my kitchen at five-thirty in the morning?'

I turned around with my tray full of scones to find him standing on the other side of the kitchen island, his hands in his pockets and his trousers half zipped. The fabric sat low on his hips, revealing golden skin and a crisp glory trail of tawny hair that had my mouth watering.

'I couldn't sleep,' I said, clearing my throat as I put the tray down on the kitchen island counter.

'So you bake?'

I'd conditioned myself not to talk about the things that excited me, but there wasn't much point in pretending to be casual about my baking. Not now there were two batches of scones sitting there.

'Yes.' I took off the oven gloves and put them on the counter next to the tray. 'I like to. Especially when I can't sleep.'

His smoky golden gaze focused on the trays of scones. 'These look…amazing.'

The simple praise warmed me like the sun on a winter's day and I couldn't help smiling. 'Thanks. I've been messing around with a recipe of my aunt's, trying to get a better rise. I think the second batch is better.'

'They all look great to me, not to mention smell bloody delicious.' He lifted a brow. 'There's jam in the fridge. And butter.'

'Was that a subtle hint?'

'It was subtle?'

I laughed, turning to get what he'd suggested from the fridge. There was whipped cream in a spray can so I grabbed that too.

When I turned back, he was in the process of grinding beans and making coffee.

'It's tea and scones, you know,' I pointed out, putting the items down on the counter.

'Not here it isn't,' he said decisively. 'Coffee. Always.'

He filled the stovetop espresso maker and put it on the element, then came back over to the counter to stand beside me. 'Why baking?' He reached for a scone. 'Seems an odd thing for a scientist to do.'

'Not really. Baking is just chemistry.'

'It is?'

'Of course. It's all about mixing things to create chemical reactions. How one ingredient works with another, or doesn't work depending on the measurement. It's fascinating how they all work together.' I warmed to my favourite subject. 'Or don't if you mess up the proportions. Or how amazing it can turn out if you add something else.'

He smiled and it wasn't the manufactured smile of a man setting out to charm, but spontaneous and full of warmth. It turned him from hot to breathtaking in a matter of seconds. 'Where did you learn to bake? Did that get you into chemistry or vice versa?'

I blushed under the warmth of that smile. 'My aunt taught me. The one I got sent away to. She thought I needed something to do. And since it was like science, with all that precise measuring, I...' I faltered, feeling silly for no good reason.

'You liked it,' he finished, that gorgeous smile curling his mouth.

My cheeks felt hot. 'Yes.'

'And you're good at it too.' He pulled the scone in his hands apart and it steamed gently, the delicious smell filling the space between us. 'My mother died when I was young,' he went on. 'I don't remember her, but I do remember the various stepmothers I had. One of them used to bake. Not often and not well, but she did. Scones were her best recipe and, though they weren't as good as these, my brothers and I used to like them.' He looked down at the scone in his hand. 'When she baked, it was like...I had a normal family.'

My breath caught at the unexpected confession. He was looking down, golden lashes veiling his expression, but I heard the wistfulness in his voice.

Part of me didn't want to speak in case I ruined the moment, but I couldn't stop myself. He'd let me have another crumb of information about himself and I was hooked.

'Is that what you wanted?' I tried to sound casual. 'A normal family?'

'Yes. Christ, I would have given anything for Dad to be a builder or an accountant or, shit, a truck driver. But he wasn't.' There was a flash of gold as he glanced at me. 'I don't know why I'm telling you this.'

I tried to keep things light. 'Because you're hungry and you want a scone, and you'll do anything to get one?'

He smiled that breathtaking smile again. 'You shouldn't get comfortable with me, Vita. And you damn well shouldn't trust me.'

The words were offered so casually I almost didn't understand. And then I did.

'Why not?' I asked, even though I didn't want to know. 'Why shouldn't I trust you?'

'You know what kind of man I am.' His gaze didn't flicker. 'I'm dangerous. I don't like being vulnerable and I hurt people who make me feel that way.'

My throat had gone dry, but I refused to admit it was fear. 'You won't hurt me.'

'Never physically, no. But you don't know me. And you don't know what I'm capable of. I might not use violence these days, but I use every other trick in the book to get people to do what my brothers and I want.' He paused, his gaze searching mine. 'I could use that video of us last night, for example.'

He won't.

The thought was instinctive and I accepted it without question. If he'd genuinely been going to use it he would have uploaded it first thing this morning, not threatened me with it first.

'But you won't.' I put all my certainty into the words. 'Because if I thought for a second you would, I wouldn't have given it to you.'

His smile faded. 'You don't know—'

This time it was my turn to put my finger over his beautiful mouth. 'You're trying very hard to convince me you're some kind of monster, Leon. And I don't know why.'

He put down the scone, gently wrapped his fingers around my wrist and tugged my finger from his mouth. 'As I was saying,' he went on as if I hadn't interrupted, 'I'll never willingly let anyone have power over me ever again.'

Again, the whisper of cold foreboding that I'd felt last night settled inside me, though I wasn't sure why.

'I understand that,' I said. 'After what happened to you, I wouldn't either.'

'No.' His voice was quiet. 'You don't understand. Once you've survived a world like my father's, protecting yourself becomes automatic. Instinctive. Because you can't ever let your guard down and you can't ever trust.'

'Yes, I get it.' I studied him. 'But you trust me, right?'

His golden gaze darkened. 'I can't, vixen. Not even you.'

CHAPTER SEVENTEEN

Leon

VITA STARED AT ME, her dark eyes wide. She was dressed only in my shirt and had a smear of flour on her cheek and a scattering of it in her hair. She looked like she'd wandered off the set of a feel-good movie starring an adorable baker heroine.

I had no idea what such a creature was doing in my kitchen, baking scones and getting flour everywhere, reminding me of happier times in my childhood and making me confess all kinds of ridiculous bullshit.

And the confessions kept on coming, things I'd never told anyone. Such as how all I'd wanted was a normal family. How I wasn't to be trusted, no matter what she thought of me.

How I would never—could never—trust her.

Her black eyes were very direct, very bright. 'Then why did you tell me all that stuff last night?'

'Because you wanted me to. Because you asked.'

She was silent for a long moment. 'You're trying to push me away, aren't you?'

She knew. She wasn't stupid.

'It's a warning,' I said. 'Don't get too close, sweetheart. And don't mess with me. I'm one experiment that might just blow up in your face.'

She bristled. 'I'm not messing with you. It's not my fault scones bring back memories you don't like.'

I'd offended her, as I'd meant to. As I'd intended. But I didn't feel pleased with myself. I felt ashamed.

All she'd done was bake her scones then shyly tell me about her love of baking, her eyes lighting up with pleasure as she'd done so.

'Baking is just chemistry', she'd said and I could see how that worked. It made me wish I'd woken earlier so I would have been able to watch her as she'd bustled about the kitchen I never used, mixing up her ingredients and creating those chemical reactions.

But that shouldn't be happening between us. She shouldn't be getting me to tell her things I'd never told anyone else. Things about myself that should stay buried. Sex was all it was, not whispered confessions and sweet kisses, and baking in the morning.

So yes, I wanted to push her away. I wanted some distance between us because it felt like she was cracking the armour I wore, putting little chinks in it, weakening it.

I couldn't let that happen but…I didn't like that I'd offended her. It made something deep inside me ache.

'I'm not a child,' she went on, her expression fierce. 'Yes, you did some bad things, and yes, you're ruthless. But I know that already. I mean, come on, Leon. Manipulating me into this marriage thing was kind of an indicator that you're not exactly pure as the driven snow.' A crease appeared between her brows as if something she hadn't thought of suddenly occurred to her. 'Actually, you were honest about that. And you didn't have to be.'

Christ. Next she'd be telling me what a hero I was.

I pushed the scone I'd pulled apart towards her. 'Why don't you put some butter and jam on this for me?'

One reddish brow rose imperiously. 'Excuse me?'

I met her gaze, steeling myself to do something I hardly ever did. 'I'm sorry,' I said and, possibly for the first time in years, I meant it. 'I know you're not a child. I just...don't want you to get hurt.'

Since when did you start caring about her feelings?

She blinked as if I'd said something unexpected. 'I won't get hurt. I can take care of myself.'

'Like you took care of yourself with Simon?'

She flushed. 'I was only seventeen. And I'm not seventeen now.' Reaching for the scone I'd pushed in her direction, she began to butter it. 'Anyway, you and me, it's just sex. That's what we agreed.' Carefully, she wiped the knife then began to spread the jam, then added, half to herself, 'A chemical reaction, that's all.'

She was right. That was exactly what we had. Nothing but chemicals.

So why do you still ache?

But I ignored that too. 'No more questions.'

'Okay, no more questions.' She lifted the scone towards me. 'But that doesn't mean we can't talk, right?'

'We can talk,' I agreed then leaned forward and bit into the scone she held.

It was the most delicious thing I'd ever eaten in my life—apart from her.

She watched me as I chewed then swallowed, her gaze drifting to my mouth.

'You've got…' She reached out to swipe away the cream on my top lip.

I grabbed her wrist, licked the rest of the cream from her finger then drew it deep into my mouth, stroking it with my tongue.

Her lips parted, her dark gaze becoming even darker as she watched me lick her finger.

'The scone was delicious,' I murmured roughly against her skin. 'But you taste even better.' Taking her finger from my mouth, I pulled her towards me. 'And I'm done talking. Care to experiment with another kind of chemical reaction, vixen?'

CHAPTER EIGHTEEN

Leon

'DO I REALLY HAVE to try these on?' Vita's voice drifted from down the hallway, sounding exasperated. 'You've left this rather late.'

I smiled at her annoyed tone, settling back against the couch cushions and glancing towards the doorway.

I'd had some wedding gowns from an exclusive bridal salon sent to my penthouse for her to try on, and, yes, I'd left it late given that the wedding was only a couple of weeks away. The rest of the organisation was in the capable hands of the wedding planner and the King Enterprises corporate events team and I was confident they'd be able to pull it off to the specifications I'd given them.

Not that I'd given them many since I didn't really care how the wedding went. As long as it was big, that was all that mattered.

I'd planned the same thing for the wedding gowns, thinking to pick one at random for Vita to wear since, again, it didn't really matter what she wore.

Then I'd changed my mind, uncomfortable with

the thought of her wearing something she might not like or that may not suit her.

I didn't think about why it was important to me that she liked her gown. I pushed that particular thought right to the back of my head.

I wanted her to like it, end of story.

A sigh came from the bedroom and I was very tempted to go in there and help her into the gown myself. Though that would probably end with us both naked and the gown on the floor. Which wasn't the point of the exercise.

I shifted on the couch, trying to ease the growing tightness in my trousers. The sweet scent of the chocolate chip cookies she'd baked earlier was still in the air, reminding me of how I'd laid her across the kitchen counter and licked melted chocolate off her body.

My cock liked that memory very much indeed.

'Hurry up, vixen,' I muttered. 'You're creating a problem.'

'What problem?' Vita asked.

My head snapped up and there she was, standing in front of me, wearing the first of three gowns. This one had a fitted bodice and frothy skirts, with a thousand crystals sewn everywhere, glittering like stardust.

And my heart did a strange thing. It felt like it… turned over.

She looked like a princess.

'What—' I had to stop and clear my throat, unable to speak. 'What do you think?'

Vita put the veil she was holding on her head then turned to the full-length mirror that I'd had brought in and set up opposite the couch.

'It's heavy.' She kicked at the skirts, frowning. 'All these crystals are a bit much.'

We both looked at her in the mirror.

'You look...lovely,' I said, unable to get rid of the husky edge to my voice.

Colour swept over her face and she gave me a smile that made my heart turn over yet again.

'Thank you.' She smoothed the skirts. 'But I feel like I'm wearing a suit of armour. I don't think it's really me.'

'It is you,' I said. 'You look like a princess.'

Again that smile. I could barely keep my hands to myself.

God, what the hell was wrong with me? It was only a wedding dress for a wedding that wasn't even real. It didn't mean anything.

'Try on the second one.' I kept my tone brusque, looking down at my phone so she couldn't see my face.

I heard her leave the room while I went over some work emails. Or tried to. Difficult when every sense I had was tuned to the sound of her in the bedroom, trying on the second gown.

I wasn't ready when I heard her come back in.

I wasn't ready when I lifted my head to look at her.

This gown was more fitting than the previous one, the skirts slimmer. There were no crystals, but there was a long train that spilled out behind her like trailing foam from a wave.

If she'd looked like a princess in the first gown, in the second she looked like a queen.

Desperately, some part of me tried to find the angles and plain features of the woman I'd met in the nightclub a couple of weeks earlier. But I couldn't find her. She was gone.

All that was left was the goddess in front of me.

She seemed oblivious to me staring at her like a fucking idiot, turning around to look at herself in the mirror again.

'This one isn't as heavy. But the train is a pain in the neck. I won't be able to walk anywhere.'

'You look amazing.' I tried to be casual, yet the words were somehow difficult. 'But yes, I wouldn't want anything getting in the way. Especially not when the time comes for me to claim my wedding night.'

She glanced at me in the mirror and I realised what I'd said. And what it meant.

A wedding night. We hadn't talked about that. About what we would do in those few months of 'blissful wedlock' before I left the country. Initially, I'd assumed I'd leave her to her own devices, but now… Would our wedding really be our last night together? It made sense to end this affair between us there. Both for my own sanity and hers. Though, how ironic. A marriage was supposed to signify a beginning, not an end.

Vita said nothing, but the light had dimmed in her dark eyes. As if she'd had the same thought and it had made her sad.

It makes you sad too.

I gritted my teeth, my jaw aching.

'Try on the last one,' I said roughly. 'That one doesn't have a train.'

She nodded and disappeared back down the hallway again.

I got out my phone once more, gripping it tightly.

Yet more emails and this time all wedding-related. Fuck, I didn't want to answer them. All I could think about was whether or not I'd insist on our wedding night as our last night together.

It had to be. Because afterwards I'd be leaving and never coming back.

You want to stay.

I scowled at my phone. No, I didn't want to stay. I couldn't. There was nothing for me here but my brothers, and they didn't need me. Xander had his numbers and Ajax his thirst for vengeance. While all I had were orders—and someone else's orders at that. I hadn't been my own man when Dad had been around and I still wasn't my own man now.

I had to go somewhere else. Start a new life where my past didn't matter. A life I chose, not one that was forced on me.

But that's not the life you want.

My chest constricted, an ache sitting just behind my breastbone, the dreams of long ago replaying in my head. Dreams of a normal family, with a husband and wife and their children. No violence. No blood. No crime.

You could have that with her.

I blinked, the ache inside me deepening.

Scones in the morning with coffee. And a lovely woman with auburn hair and flour on her cheek, wearing my shirt and smiling as she wiped cream from my lip. Blushing as I licked it from her finger then drew her close. Telling me that she trusted me…

No. It was a life I'd never had. A dream that wasn't meant for me.

Because to have it I'd have to care. I'd have to take

my armour off, be vulnerable and give the power to someone else. And I couldn't. Caring was the end of you. The cut you couldn't heal from. The real torture.

All those cigarette burns, those knife wounds, they weren't the things that hurt. The agony came from knowing no one had come for me, not even my own father. I was expendable, unneeded. My life not even worth the ransom money they'd tried to extort from him.

I would never leave myself open to that again.

I heard her footfall as she came back and this time I waited before I looked, pretending I was more interested in what was on my phone to cover the beating of my heart and the rush of blood in my veins.

'Leon,' she said.

I had to force myself to look.

The third gown was the simplest of all. It was ivory satin that followed her every curve, the same way I followed them with my hands every night. The fabric gathered at one shoulder in a Grecian style before falling gracefully down her back.

In the first two gowns she'd looked like royalty, like a fairy tale.

But in this one, all simplicity and elegance, she looked like herself.

Bright. Passionate. Honest.

My heart didn't turn over this time. It stood still.

She'd taken her hair down and it curled over her shoulders in an auburn tumble, and I could see exactly how she should wear it for the wedding. Either loose or in a long braid, and there should be flowers woven through it, simple white flowers to accentuate the lovely colour.

'What about this one?' she asked, hesitant.

She wanted me to like it, I could see by the look on her face.

The reply I'd been going to make—something dismissive to hide my own reaction to her—died unsaid. I couldn't bring myself to say it.

It's too late to protect yourself. Too late to pretend you don't care.

I shut that voice off. Hard. Then I put my phone away and I got up from the couch. And I moved over to where she stood, letting my gaze roam over her, from the top of her red head down to her feet, lingering on my favourite places—her breasts, her hips, the swell of her thighs and her elegant calves and ankles.

Then I lifted my attention to her face, staring into her dark eyes, watching those stars twinkle brightly in the velvety blackness.

She could be yours. Your wife. You could have scones and coffee and her. You could have the family you always wanted.

My heart twisted painfully.

I'd met many dangerous people in my life, but suddenly I knew that the woman standing in front of me right now was the most dangerous of the lot.

She had the power to destroy me if I let her.

'Yes.' I fought to keep my expression neutral. 'That's the one.'

She blushed, giving me a smile that had my heart restarting, battering against my ribs like a prisoner trying to escape a cell.

'I think I like it.' She turned back to the mirror. 'It feels much lighter and it's easier to move around in.'

It was difficult to speak. Like someone had their hand around my throat and was squeezing.

To cover my reaction, I took the end of the length of fabric that fell down her back. 'I wonder what would happen if I pulled this…?'

'Don't you dare.' She moved away, then turned to give me a mock stern look. 'It's not our wedding night yet.'

All she was doing was standing there. With bare feet and her hair loose around her shoulders. Dressed in ivory satin.

I wanted her so badly I couldn't speak.

Lust, that was all it was. Nothing to do with her telling me how good I was for her or how she trusted me. Nothing to do with the way she looked at me, as if my past didn't matter. As if she saw a man worth looking at.

Nothing to do with that at all.

I grabbed her, pulling her up against me.

Her eyes went wide and she put her hands on my chest. 'What is it?'

I was breathing very fast, like I couldn't get enough air.

In a couple of weeks all this would be over. I'd be leaving the country a few months after that. I'd be giving her up and that was a good thing. A very good thing.

'Nothing.' I managed to force the words out. 'You're just really fucking sexy in that dress.'

But those bright eyes, they saw through me. 'Leon.' Her voice was quiet. 'Tell me.'

The satin of her gown felt slippery beneath my fingers, my grip on her tenuous. 'I don't want to let you go,' I heard myself say hoarsely. 'I don't want our wedding night to be the last night. I want to keep you.'

She blinked in shock and I thought for a moment I saw tears in her eyes. Then she blinked again and lifted her hands to my jaw, her fingers cool against my skin. 'So keep me.'

'I can't.'

'You can.' The words sounded husky, a fierce glow lighting her gaze. 'You don't have to let me go. I don't want you to.'

'But that's why I can't.' I stared down into her lovely face. 'You want more and I don't. So I have to let you go. I have to protect you.'

Her throat moved. 'Protect yourself, you mean.'

I didn't deny it. 'I have to, Vita.'

By rights she should have got angry, but it wasn't anger I saw in her gaze now. It was something softer, something almost tender. 'It wasn't your fault, you know,' she said quietly. 'That he didn't come for you. He should have fought for you, protected you. The way my father should have protected me.'

I wanted to tell her it didn't matter, that I didn't care, but the words wouldn't come. With a couple of simple sentences, she'd shattered my goddamn armour in two and I wasn't sure I could repair it.

So I did the only thing I could.

I turned around and walked away.

CHAPTER NINETEEN

Vita

THE DOOR OF the limo opened and I took a breath, trying not to fuss with the skirts of my gown, my fingers bunching the fabric.

A large male hand came over mine and gently pressed it down.

'You'll be fine,' Leon said calmly. 'Don't forget that your fiancé is the most dangerous man in the room and he'll punch anyone who dares to even look at you funny.'

The warmth of his hand was reassuring and I felt my nervousness ease.

I tried to be stern. 'No, you wouldn't.'

'I would.' There was a feral gleam in his golden eyes. A glimpse of the lieutenant he'd once been.

I shivered, and not because I didn't like the thought of a man offering to do violence on my behalf. I did like it. No one had stood up for me when that video went live. No one had defended me. I'd been sent away in disgrace instead. The thought of Leon protecting me gave me a delicious thrill, as if I'd somehow tamed a vicious predator.

'That appeals to you, doesn't it?' Leon observed lazily.

'Yes.' No reason to deny it. 'I feel like I've tamed a lion.'

Surprise flickered across his beautiful face. 'A lion?'

I looked at him lounging beside me, ridiculously handsome in the perfectly tailored tux he was wearing for tonight's function. 'You're all…' I gestured at him '…golden and commanding and dangerous.'

One of his rare genuine smiles curved his mouth. 'You better believe it, sweetheart. And all it took to tame me was scones, sex and chemistry. Maybe you should write a seduction "How to".'

I grinned, an odd excitement fizzing in my chest.

Then I remembered something I'd been trying hard not to over the past week.

Tonight was our last date before the wedding.

The excitement inside me died, leaving me feeling flat and stale, like a bottle of champagne that hadn't been corked properly.

A week had passed since that day I'd tried on wedding dresses in his apartment. I shouldn't have said anything then and I knew it. But the moment he'd said he wanted to keep me a stupid burst of hope had ignited inside me. And I'd opened my big fat mouth and told him that he could before I could stop myself.

I shouldn't have. I shouldn't have said a word, but I had. And then I'd made things worse when he'd refused me by handing him a truth he hadn't asked for and plainly didn't want to hear.

He'd walked out, leaving me standing there in the lovely wedding dress I'd felt so good in, knowing I'd made a huge mistake.

We'd told each other that sex was all it was, yet in that moment we'd both crossed over that boundary. Which couldn't happen.

I couldn't want more because he couldn't give it to me.

We were volatile compounds that shouldn't mix outside a controlled environment or else we'd destroy each other.

When he'd returned later that night with a bouquet of beautiful orchids and taken me to bed without a word I didn't push.

I pretended it hadn't happened.

We'd had other dates since then where we'd talked about everything else. Politics and art. Science and books. Our favourite movies and TV shows. Anything. Everything.

Everything but the chemistry between us. A chemistry that showed no signs of burning out, no matter how many dates we went on, no matter how many times he took me to bed.

And that made it so hard to pretend.

He made it so hard to pretend.

'Hey.' His fingers brushed my cheek in a light caress. 'You look sad. What's up?'

Damn. Why did he have to be so observant? Or, rather, why couldn't I be better at hiding my feelings?

I forced a smile. 'Nothing. Just nervous.'

'Like I said, nothing to be nervous about.' He grinned, the dangerous gleam in his eyes only enhancing his charisma. God, he was so hot I could hardly stand it. 'You look utterly lovely. The dress is perfect.'

I blushed.

He'd taken me shopping the day before to find me

something to wear for this charity function of my father's. It was black tie all the way, and I had nothing suitable.

Dad had never invited me to his parties—before my video I'd been too young and after he hadn't wanted me anywhere near potential donors—but tonight he'd told me that my presence was required, as was Leon's. He was going to give his public blessing to our marriage, aka introducing Leon to some potential investors.

I hated parties but I couldn't refuse this one. It was required as part of my role as Leon's fiancée. The dress was sexy, wrapping around my figure while leaving one shoulder bare. The colour suited me and I was amazed at how good I felt in it.

'Thank you,' I said. 'For the dress.' And then, because I wanted him to know, I went on, 'For the dates too. Thank you for...' For making me feel good about myself. For making me feel beautiful. For making me feel special for the first time in my life. 'For everything.'

His smile was warm, real. The smile that was just mine.

It made my heart turn over in my chest.

'You're welcome.' He kissed my palm. 'Come on, vixen. Now that we're a few minutes late we can make a grand entrance.'

I grimaced. 'Not sure I want a grand entrance.'

His fingers closed around mine. 'Sweetheart, when you're with me all entrances are grand.'

The gleam in his eyes had turned from dangerous to wicked and my stupid heart turned over yet again.

You're falling for him.

* * *

The venue for the charity function was an old historic building that was in the process of being revitalised.

Outside, the building's elegant façade remained untouched and it wasn't until we got inside that I realised the whole thing had been gutted in preparation for rebuilding.

It was an amazing space, brick walls soaring high right up to the roof, no ceilings in the way. A temporary wooden floor had been put down for the night, the lighting lots of bare old-fashioned bulbs hanging down on industrial wires. They looked like tiny moons or planets, the light they gave off diffuse and warm.

At one end a chamber orchestra played while a bar had been set up at the other. Couches and chairs in various different configurations were scattered everywhere, while on some of the walls big screens displayed logos of the charity the function was in aid of.

The place was packed with the cream of Sydney high society, all of them talking raucously, but if I'd hoped to slip in unnoticed I was disappointed.

The moment Leon walked in, his arm around my waist, there seemed to be a lull in the hum of voices. Heads turned in our direction, following our progress as we made our way through the press of people to where my father stood, ready to greet us.

I felt the weight of those stares but, unlike a couple of weeks ago, it didn't bother me the way it had on those first couple of dates.

In fact, I relished it. Because here I was, the 'I Love You Girl', in a spectacular dress with an incredibly handsome man on her arm. A man with a dangerous past who was clearly possessive and obviously besotted with her.

It was intoxicating, powerful.

As we approached my father, I lifted my chin and met his gaze, for once not afraid of the disapproval I saw in his eyes whenever he looked at me.

That disapproval was evident now but this time I let it slide off me, smiling instead.

'Tom,' Leon said expansively, stopping in front of my father and reaching out to shake his hand. 'Good to see you.'

My father's smile looked forced, his handshake stiff. 'King.'

'Oh, come now, you're my soon-to-be father-in-law. Don't you think it's time you called me Leon?' He grinned, not at all put off by Dad's wooden formality. 'We're almost family.'

Dad didn't reply, his smile remaining fixed. He turned to me instead and for a second I thought I was going to get a handshake from him too, but at the last minute he stepped up and gave me a kiss on the cheek.

'Vita,' he murmured.

'Dad.' I didn't offer a hug. He wouldn't have wanted it anyway.

He stepped back, studying my face, though what he was looking for I had no idea. 'Are you…okay?' he asked tentatively.

The question surprised me since he'd never been interested in my well-being before.

'Of course,' I said. 'Why wouldn't I be?'

'He's worried I might be corrupting you,' Leon murmured, pulling me closer, his mouth brushing my ear. 'He's right. I am.'

Dad frowned, looking from Leon to me and then back again, noting how close we were and Leon's proprietorial arm around my waist.

The frown deepened.

He wouldn't have known that Leon and I had been sleeping together. But now he did. And he wasn't happy about it.

A bolt of satisfaction shot through me and I let myself lean against Leon's tall, muscular body, my hand coming down to rest over his on my stomach. I smiled at my father.

'Are you worried about me, Dad?' I met his gaze squarely. 'Because promising me to a complete stranger didn't seem to bother you before.'

I don't know why I said it because I wasn't here to fight. In fact, I thought I'd long since given up caring what Dad thought of me. Yet now the little dig was out I didn't want to take it back.

I was conscious of Leon beside me, his arm a reassuring weight around my waist. He didn't say a word; he knew this was my fight, not his.

Dad scowled. 'Of course I'm worried about you. The Kings are—' He stopped, his gaze flicking to Leon.

'The Kings are what?' Leon's voice held a dangerous undertone.

My father shifted on his feet, looking uncomfortable. 'It's nothing. Forget I said anything.'

'I can't speak for the King family,' I said, unwilling to let it go. 'But I can speak for Leon. And I can tell you he's been nothing but kind and respectful towards me.' I paused. 'Unlike some other people in this room.'

Dad flushed, a spark of anger in his gaze.

Good. I'd wanted to goad him and I had.

'If you're implying—'

'What? Am I implying that you haven't treated me with either kindness or respect? Yes. I am.'

It wasn't the right time and this wasn't the place for a family argument, but seeing him turn his habitual expression of disapproval on Leon and talk about the Kings in a disparaging tone made me angry. That Leon deserved it for blackmailing Dad into giving me to him didn't matter.

What mattered was that Leon had been good to me and I wasn't going to stand for anyone badmouthing him.

'Vita,' he began.

But I was on a roll and I didn't let him finish. 'Leon has been nothing but good to me, Dad. He's certainly treated me better than you or Mum ever did, and I won't hear a bad word spoken about him.'

'He blackmailed me,' Dad said through gritted teeth. 'He—'

'And you promised me to a complete stranger to save yourself from your own bad debts.' I kept my voice low so no one would overhear, but I didn't hide the ferocity I felt. 'You sacrificed me to save yourself, just like you did the last time.'

Dad didn't say a word this time, staring at me in stony silence.

I'd never confronted him about his behaviour towards me all those years ago, but now I had, I couldn't seem to stop.

'I should never have agreed,' I went on. 'But I did. Because I thought you'd finally see me as your daughter instead of a stain on the family name.'

'I didn't—'

'No. I don't want to hear your justifications. But you should know that I'm not marrying Leon for you. I'm marrying him for me. Understand?'

Utter silence fell.

Leon was silent beside me while Dad simply stared at me.

He wouldn't understand. He wouldn't know what Leon had said to me about rewriting my own story. But that was okay. I wasn't going to explain it to him. I'd said what I'd needed to say, let him know that what he'd done to me all those years ago had hurt. And that I wasn't going to let him emotionally blackmail me into doing anything for him again.

It was Leon who broke the silence in the end.

'In future, I think it's best if you don't cross my beautiful fiancée.' The smile he gave Dad was hard-edged and sharp. 'Now, isn't it time you introduced my brothers and me to some of your important friends?'

CHAPTER TWENTY

Leon

I'D SEEN AJAX and Xander enter the building as Vita gave her father the dressing-down he so richly deserved, and he swung round now to watch them approach.

But I didn't pay any attention to them.

I could only look at her.

The fierce expression on her face remained and her dark eyes were glowing with anger. But for once it wasn't aimed at me; it was aimed at her father. On her own behalf, yet also, strangely, on mine.

Ah, Christ, she shouldn't say things like that. She shouldn't come to my defence, making me admire the sheer guts of her, how she was calling her father out in the middle of his own function.

I'd thought she couldn't get under my skin any more than she had already.

I was wrong.

But I couldn't let it.

Over the past week or so, since the day she'd tried on wedding dresses, I'd gone on as if I hadn't told her that I wanted to keep her.

As if she hadn't seen right through me and told me that it was myself I was protecting.

I'd simply gone on as if nothing had happened and that had worked. She hadn't mentioned it again. And the dates had continued and so had the nights, and I'd thought I was good. That I'd patched up my armour, that it was strong.

But her doing shit like this? Defending me against her father? It only made me aware that I had to be stronger. That I had to try harder.

That, no matter how well protected I thought I was, it wasn't enough.

If I'd had my way I would have ended the affair the day I'd seen her in that wedding dress, but I'd made a promise to my brother. And that promise meant keeping up this deception. Marrying her to legitimise the King name and get us into the luxury apartment market.

I couldn't let Ajax down, not after what he'd done for me.

What about her?

I ignored the question, turning instead to greet my brothers as they came through the crowd towards us.

They'd been sent invites to this little show, their presence required so Hamilton could introduce us to his high-flying friends.

Ajax was a huge hulking figure in jeans, a T-shirt and a leather jacket—the man had no goddamn sense of occasion—while Xander, not quite as tall but no less broad, had at least made an effort and put on a tux.

Both of them kept glancing at Vita, making me instinctively pull her closer.

Staking your claim?

Well, she was mine, at least for now, and I wanted to make sure my brothers knew it. Ajax, particularly, was rapacious in his tastes and, as for Xander... Though his interests lay with protecting his money, if he thought Vita was a threat to us he wouldn't hesitate to make that known. In ways that would be painful for all concerned.

'Ajax, Xander,' I said as they stopped in front of us. 'Meet your future sister-in-law, Vita Hamilton.'

Ajax turned his disturbing light blue stare from me to Vita, the look on his face unreadable. 'A pleasure.' His voice was neutral as he held out a hand to her.

Vita took it and instantly every instinct I had went on high alert.

I didn't like her touching him. I didn't like him touching her.

You're a fucking lost cause.

I crushed the thought. Since telling Vita not to shake my brother's hand would look strange, I didn't say a word but I kept a close eye on Ajax, resisting the urge to knock his hand away.

'Hello,' Vita said gravely. 'Nice to meet you too.'

Ajax nodded, holding on to her hand for a second too long, making me nearly growl my displeasure. His gaze flicked to mine and I swear I caught amusement there.

He was messing with me, the bastard.

I bared my teeth at him, in no mood for games.

Xander, meanwhile, shook Vita's hand while his dark gaze ran over her, coldly measuring and assessing. He didn't say a word, not even a hello.

'Your manners are beautiful as always, Xander.' My tone was acid as he dropped Vita's hand like it had burned him. I reached for it instead, threading my fingers through hers, and when I felt hers tighten around mine I felt warmth spread out in my chest.

I ignored the sensation as I turned to Hamilton. He was struggling to hide his disapproval—now I knew where Vita had got her bad acting skills from.

'You know my brothers, don't you?' I said pleasantly. 'Though, of course, they need no introduction.' I smiled. 'Now, you're going to introduce us around, aren't you? Let everyone know how happy you are that I'm going to be part of your family. So happy and excited that you're to share the plans King Enterprises has for a new luxury apartment complex, hmm?'

Hamilton hated that; I could see it in his eyes. And he hated me too, which was not surprising. Not when I held all the cards.

Too bad. Perhaps if he'd been a better father to Vita and less of an arrogant bastard, I might have felt more lenient towards him. But he wasn't, so I didn't.

'Yes, of course,' Hamilton said through gritted teeth. 'Please excuse us, Vita. I'll show the Kings around.'

We made the rounds of the room, Hamilton introducing us to his high society cronies, but I found myself unable to pay attention. I kept looking in Vita's direction, checking to make sure she was okay. I knew she hadn't been looking forward to this, not with all the people, and I wanted to check that no one was hassling her or giving her grief. But she was smiling, obviously enjoying the conversation she was having with some prick in an overly fancy tux.

I didn't like it.

I should have been focusing on Hamilton and the

people he was introducing us to, on the conversations that were happening all around me. I should have been taking part, using my charm to get those potential investors on our side. But for some reason that didn't seem very important right now.

What was important was that some bastard was standing next to Vita and obviously flirting with her.

My Vita.

So much for her being only a chemical reaction.

There was a pressure in my chest, a tightness I couldn't ignore. I'd never been jealous before and there was no reason for me to be so now. Maybe it was simply because we didn't have much longer together before the wedding and I wanted to spend that time with her.

Or maybe no one touches what's yours?

But she wasn't mine and I didn't want her to be.

Across the room, another man had joined the first standing next to Vita and she smiled at him too. Then, as I watched, that smile faded and her face went white, and it felt like a bomb had exploded in my chest.

'Excuse me,' I murmured to Ajax as Hamilton presented us to yet another rich bastard who looked at us as if we were dirt. 'I have something I need to attend to.'

Ajax frowned. 'What? You need to—'

But I'd already turned away, threading my way quickly through the crowd to where Vita stood. A bright stain of colour stood out on her white cheeks and there was a fixed smile on her face. She was trying to pretend she was okay, but she wasn't.

That fucking bastard had said something to hurt her, I was certain.

You're not supposed to care.

No, I wasn't. Not caring was how I got through my entire fucking life. And yet I couldn't seem to not care about Vita.

I headed straight towards her and she noticed me approaching. Her eyes widened, the tiny stars in them flaring with what looked like relief. And that hit me like a punch to the gut, made the pressure in my chest increase as if someone had dumped a large and heavy stone directly on it.

She needed me.

It made something deep inside me crack.

I slid an arm around her waist as I got to her, pulling her in tight against me before rounding on the two pricks standing near her.

I smiled at them with teeth and fury, giving them a glimpse of the lieutenant. And, much to my satisfaction, both of them went as white as Vita had.

'It appears my fiancée is in some distress.' My voice was barely above a snarl. 'What did you say to her?'

Instantly, they began making excuses, falling over themselves to assure me they hadn't said a word, and besides, they'd only been joking.

'If either of you have hurt her,' I interrupted pleasantly, 'I will kill you. Understand?'

And I meant it. I meant every goddamn word.

'Leon,' Vita murmured.

I turned sharply, taking my arm from around her so I could cup her face between my palms. 'They hurt you. What did they say?' Fury ran hot in my veins, and along with it, the need for violent punishment. 'I meant it. I'll fucking kill them if they—'

'No,' she said quietly but firmly. 'It was nothing.'

'It wasn't nothing. I saw you go white.'

And she still was. But her gaze was very calm, very direct. 'He only made some comment about the video and I wasn't expecting it.'

I snarled, ready to let her go and turn on the assholes who'd hurt her, everything in me wanting to deal them back in kind. But her hands came over mine where they rested on her jaw, holding them there. 'Don't. You don't need to do anything. You came to support me and that's enough.'

'But you—'

'I thanked him for his comment and told him that if he liked the earlier video, he should see the one I made with you.'

My heart was beating fast, adrenaline pumping hard in my veins, and I wanted to do violence. Yet there was apparently room in me for admiration. Shit, this woman…

'Are you saying you didn't need me to defend your honour?' I tried to make it sound like a joke, except it didn't come out like one.

She smiled, a faint curl of her lovely mouth, as if she'd heard the desperate note in my voice. 'No, but I'm glad you came back anyway.'

Of course she didn't need me. She was strong—much stronger than she gave herself credit for.

The pressure on my chest felt suffocating all of a sudden, desire and an inexplicable desperation filling me. I wanted to be somewhere private, somewhere I could show her that she did need me. Somewhere I could make her as desperate as I was now.

I was supposed to be keeping distance between us, yet right now that felt impossible.

I leaned down so we were nose to nose. 'Come with me.'

She gave me a surprised look. 'Why? Where are we going?'

I gave her the only response I was able, bending to kiss her hungrily right there in the middle of the crowded party. In front of everyone.

She didn't protest. Didn't resist. Her mouth opened beneath mine immediately, the sweet taste of her filling me.

But it wasn't enough.

It's never going to be enough.

The whisper in my head was insidious and I ignored it. Releasing her, I stepped back then took her hand. 'Come on. Let's go.'

As I strode towards the exit with Vita I could see my brothers on the far side of the room, shaking hands and making nice. Or at least as nice as they'd ever get. They needed me to smooth the way since neither of them were exactly good with people. Ajax was too impatient and Xander was too cold.

I should be with them but Vita's hand was in mine and I couldn't let her go. I just…needed some time with her, to get rid of this desperation, and then maybe I'd come back and do what I was supposed to do.

Ajax was staring at me, frowning. But I didn't stop.

Later. I'd make this up to them later.

Outside, I texted the limo driver and within five minutes he had the limo waiting at the kerb.

'Are you okay?' Vita asked as I hustled her inside it. 'I'm not hurt, really.'

Fuck. What had I given away? And more importantly, how had she noticed? Not that I wasn't okay. Of course I was.

I put my hand behind her neck and pulled her forward, taking her mouth again, stopping any conversation.

Her taste filled me once again and I thought it would calm me, but it didn't. It only made me more desperate.

This was crazy. Fucking crazy. What was wrong with me?

I'd tried to protect her, but she hadn't needed it, and that should make me glad, not make me feel like I was trying to hold on to something that kept slipping through my fingers.

I'd walked out on my brothers during an important function. And all because a woman was suddenly more important to me than the promise I'd made to Ajax. More important than the King name.

It was insane. I should tell her it was a mistake, get out of the car and go back to what I was supposed to be doing.

Yet I didn't.

I spread my fingers over the back of her neck, tightening my hold, pushing my tongue into her hot, sweet mouth. Kissing her hard and deep. Letting her know who she needed, no matter how much she told me she didn't.

Me.

'Leon,' she murmured against my lips, her hands coming to my chest and pushing. 'Not here.'

But I was rapidly passing the point of no return.

My cock ached. Everything ached. I needed to be inside her now.

Pulling away, I leaned forward to mutter some instructions to the driver, then I stabbed the button that raised the partition between us and the front seats.

I shouldn't give in to this feeling. I should try and master it, not let it master me. Not let it feel like it was breaking something inside me.

Or maybe I should find some other woman to help me deal with it, one who didn't get under my skin or leave me feeling like I couldn't breathe.

But even the thought of another woman left me cold.

It was Vita I wanted.

It was Vita I had to have any way I could.

My brain tried to insist that this was a dumb idea, but I was past caring what my stupid fucking brain thought.

You care and you know what happens when you care.

Caring was a weakness and when you became weak you became a target. Easy to manipulate. Easy to betray.

Hadn't I learned that? Hadn't Thompson used my hope that my dad would come for me against me? He'd tortured me with the fact that Dad wouldn't pay the ransom simply for his own amusement. Making me feel insignificant, expendable. And all because I'd cared that Dad wouldn't come.

Because I'd thought he loved me.

Christ, I needed to stop this. Get back to the function. Do the things I'd promised my brothers I'd do.

Instead, I put my arm around Vita and pulled her in close again, burying my fingers in her hair and pulling her head back. Bending to kiss her exposed throat, bite her. Taste her skin. Mark her. Get her flavour and her scent all over me and mine all over her.

She shuddered, gasping as I bit her, then I tensed as she raised her hands. But she didn't push me away again. One hand crept around the back of my neck, her thumb stroking my skin, while the other threaded into my hair, holding on as tight to me as I was to her.

I bit her again, not gently, relishing her tremble and shiver. Then I pulled the golden gown from her shoulder.

She wasn't wearing a bra underneath so there was nothing to stop me from taking one small round breast in my palm. Her skin was hot and silky, her nipple hard.

'Leon,' she murmured, shuddering again as I circled the tip of her breast with my thumb. 'The driver…'

'The partition is up. We'll be stopping soon.'

Then I covered her mouth again before she could reply, licking my way inside, wanting her sweetness and heat. Kissing her deeply, completely. As if she was mine.

Because she was.

All of her was mine.

I didn't question the rightness of the thought, merely angling her head back to give me greater access to her mouth while I stroked and teased her hardened nipple. She panted, arching up into my hand, her hold on the back of my neck tightening.

The car had stopped moving, which meant the driver had done what I'd instructed and parked in the underground car park of my apartment building. The door slammed, indicating he'd got out.

Excellent.

I'd planned to whisk her upstairs and have her in my bed, but there wasn't time. I couldn't wait.

I sat back against the seat, pulling her into my lap so she was astride me, facing me. Then I tugged her skirts up around her waist, freeing her legs, urging her forward so her knees were spread wide and that hot little pussy of hers was positioned over my hard dick.

I looked into her eyes as I reached down and tugged aside the fabric of her underwear, and I kept on looking as I stroked through her silky folds, all hot and slick against my fingers.

Desire was in her eyes, but a crease had also appeared between her reddish brows. I knew that crease. I'd seen it whenever something puzzled her.

Too bad. If she wanted to know what was happening to me, I had no answer to give her. Because I didn't know myself.

I only knew that if I didn't get inside her right now I was going to explode.

'Leon.' Her voice caught as I slid a finger inside her. 'W-what's...wrong? Something is.'

'The only thing that's wrong is that I'm not in your pussy yet.' I slipped another finger into her damp heat and her head fell back, a groan escaping her. 'Are you ready, vixen?' I spread my fingers out, feeling her wetness and the tight clasp of her sex. 'Are you ready to take me?'

Her hands came to my shoulders, holding on tight. 'Yes.'

I didn't wait. I clawed at my trousers and got them undone. Then I took my cock out, gripping her hips and positioning myself.

I thrust up into her, hot and slick, feeling her grip

on my shoulders tighten. Listening to her sharp gasp of pleasure. Watching her eyes, dark as midnight, get even darker.

I thought being inside her would help, would ease the ache in my chest and the desperation that had sunk its claws into me.

But it didn't. If anything it got worse.

She was so close to me, and I was inside her, the wet heat of her pussy wrapped like a glove around my dick.

Yet it felt like there was still a distance between us. A distance I should have been keeping and yet now couldn't stand. A distance I wanted to close.

I pulled at the gown, tugging the material down until she was bare to the waist, the gold fabric bunched around her hips. But I didn't care. I slid my arms around her, caressing her spine, urging her to lean back. She did so, her breasts firm and ripe near my mouth.

Bending, I flicked one stiff little nipple with my tongue, feeling her tremble, hearing her moan. Then I shifted, gripping her tight as I thrust up into her. I kept on teasing her nipple, sucking on it, biting it as I moved inside her, deep, slow strokes designed to drive us both mad.

Except I was the one going mad.

I was deep inside her, the pleasure of it intense. I couldn't get closer than this, yet why did it feel like I needed more?

Sliding my hands up her back, I buried them in her hair and held on tight as I moved, looking into her dark eyes as if the answer to that question was there for me to read.

Yet all I could see was desire and a rising concern that I knew would kill the mood if I let it. So I didn't let it.

I moved, taking her down onto the seat and pushing her onto her back. Then I began to drive myself into her, deep, hard, fast. As if I could fuck the hunger and desperation right out of my system, drown us both in pleasure.

She wrapped her legs around my waist, her fingers digging into my shoulders as she lifted her hips to match my movements. The air was full of the sound of our gasps and the thick, musky scents of sex and sweat. The windows were fogging, the car rocking as I fucked her harder, deeper, slamming her into the seat beneath me.

Pleasure was blinding me. She was too hot, too tight, too much of everything. Yet even this, even with her wrapped around me, half naked, her breasts bouncing and shivering every time I thrust into her, it wasn't enough.

Her eyes were black as they looked into mine, yet full of those bright stars. And I wanted to fall into that velvet darkness. It would be so soft, warm, welcoming.

'Vita.' Her name was magic on my tongue and I slid one hand between us, finding her clit and pressing down.

I felt the moment she came, her pussy clenching tight around me, saw it flash like a comet in her eyes. She cried out, the sound echoing around the car, and it was only then I let myself go.

Getting in as deep as I could, I braced myself over her, watching her as I moved.

She was staring up at me as if she'd never seen

me before in her life and I had no idea what she saw. But when she reached up and touched my cheek I felt something inside me crack right through.

'Lion,' she murmured, her voice a husky whisper. 'My lion.'

I had no idea what she meant, but then it didn't matter because the pleasure that licked up my spine was starting to take me apart piece by aching piece, stealing my awareness of everything but her beneath me and the silky wet velvet of her pussy holding me tight.

The orgasm swept over me, a tide of raw ecstasy that reached out and pulled me under.

And my last thought was that if this was simply a chemical reaction then why did it make me feel like I had a chest full of broken glass?

CHAPTER TWENTY-ONE

Vita

LEON'S BREATHING WAS fast and hard in the silence of the car. He was lying heavily on me, but I didn't mind. His weight covering me made me feel inexplicably safe and cared for. Protected.

He'd turned his head into my neck and I could feel his breath against my skin. It made me shiver. He was still deep inside me and I had my legs wrapped tightly around him as if I wanted to keep him there.

I'd told myself we had to stay separate from one another—each compound safe in its own test tube—but now… Something was wrong and I didn't know what it was.

He'd told me he couldn't keep me, that he couldn't care about me, and yet back there at the function he'd stalked towards me radiating menace, a kind of lethal intent that promised retribution of the worst kind. He'd put himself between me and the two guys as if he'd wanted to shield me and keep me safe. Then he'd taken me out into the car, seeming half feral, claiming me with an insistence that bordered on desperation.

It didn't make any sense.

If he didn't care, why had he wanted to protect me? And why had he then taken me so desperately?

I lifted my hands instead and touched his hair, pushing my fingers through the thick, soft tawny silk. He was still breathing very fast, golden lashes veiling his gaze.

Had it been because I'd dealt with those guys myself? That I'd told him I didn't need him to protect me? But, if so, why had that made him desperate? And what was he desperate about?

Perhaps it's you.

But I didn't want to go down that path, not when it didn't lead anywhere. And reading anything into his behaviour would be a mistake. This affair might feel real to me, but it wasn't. He'd told me so himself.

Something ached deep inside me, but I couldn't afford to pay any attention to it so I didn't.

I let my fingers play through his hair, focusing only on the moment, his body on mine and the feel of him still buried deep inside me. He was getting hard again.

He shifted all of a sudden, pushing himself up. 'No condom,' he said thickly. 'I forgot.'

'It's okay. I started on the Pill, remember?' I'd begun taking it when we'd first started sleeping together since condoms alone weren't fail-safe.

An expression I couldn't name flashed over his face then was gone. He turned away, pulling out of me before moving down one end of the car seat and carefully tucking himself away.

I sat up, conscious that my gown was a crumpled mess bunched around my waist and that I was just about naked, my breasts bare, my knickers pulled to one side.

He wasn't looking at me and that made me feel awkward. I began to set my clothing to rights. Usually he helped me with it, but he didn't now, running one hand through his hair then pulling at the sleeves of his jacket.

The silence in the car felt heavy. Thick.

Something was very, very wrong.

'Did…' I began, then my voice cracked and I had to start again. 'Did I…do something?'

He shot me a look. 'What do you mean?'

'You're very quiet. I wondered if I'd done something wrong.'

'No. You haven't.' He put his hand on the door handle. 'I'll get the driver to take you home.'

My stomach lurched. Normally he'd take me upstairs to his apartment.

'You're sending me away?' I couldn't mask the quiver that crept into my voice. 'I thought you wanted to be alone with me?'

'And I have been.' His expression was taut, his eyes glittering. 'But it would be better if you went home now.'

'Why?' Hurt bloomed inside me. 'Leon, you need to tell me if I did—'

'I can't.' He cut me off, his voice suddenly hard. 'I can't do this with you any more.'

It took a moment for my brain to process what he'd said.

The expression on his beautiful face was like granite and just as cold.

'I don't understand.' I tried to make the words sound as level as I could. 'Can't do what with me any more?'

'I can't continue sleeping with you. It's for the best

anyway. The wedding will be in a couple of days and then eventually I'll be leaving for good.' He gave me a hideous forced smile. 'Better to end on a high note.'

'Sex in a limo is the high note?'

'Sex anywhere is a high note.' He pulled at his jacket again, paying special attention to the sleeves. 'I'm sorry, Vita. But I have a lot to do to get ready for leaving Sydney.'

I didn't know where I got my courage from. But maybe standing up to my father and that guy who'd made the rude comment had enabled me to find some backbone because a rush of anger filled me.

Ignoring my own fears, I reached out and grabbed Leon's chin, turning his face towards me.

'No,' I said furiously. 'You don't get to do this. You don't get to pull me away from Dad's party like you can't get enough of me, have me in the back seat of your limo because you can't wait, then tell me it's over. Like it meant nothing to you. Like I mean nothing to you.' I could feel the tension in his muscles but I didn't let go of him, staring into his hot golden eyes. 'Don't treat me like that, Leon. Don't treat me like Simon did. Don't make me feel like dirt. I deserve better than that from you.'

He stared at me, unmoving. Then suddenly he grabbed my wrist and held on to it, his fingers pressing against my skin.

'I can't care about you, Vita,' he said harshly and abruptly. 'I told you that already. I can't. I won't.'

The lurching sensation in my gut got worse, which was strange since I knew this.

'I'm not asking you to care about me,' I insisted. 'Sex only—that's what we agreed and I'm fine with it.'

His amber gaze was unreadable. 'Well, I'm not.'

'What do you mean you're not?' I struggled to understand. 'You mean you're not fine with it being sex only? But I thought that's what you wanted?'

'I thought it was what I wanted too. But you're right.' His gaze focused intently on me. 'You do deserve better than that.'

'But I don't—'

'You deserve more than just sex—far more. You're honest and scarily intelligent. You're bright, beautiful and brave. And you deserve someone who can match you. Someone who cares about you. Someone who can give you what you need.'

I stared at him, bewildered. 'But I never said anything about wanting more. Or needing more.'

Strangely, his gaze softened. As if he could see things inside me that I couldn't see myself. 'You might not think you do. But you deserve it all the same.'

There was a lump in my throat, making it feel sore and dry.

'What about you?' I shot back. 'Don't you need more than that too? Don't you deserve it?'

'Sweetheart. I'm the last person in the world who deserves anything at all.'

There was something bleak in the words and in the expression on his face. It made my heart ache.

He thought of himself as bad, I already knew that. Untrustworthy and irredeemable. But that hadn't been my experience of him. Sure, he was arrogant and manipulative and way too sure of himself. But there was also a kindness in him that he kept cleverly hidden. A kindness that in the past week had become more apparent as he'd taken me out on those dates, turning them from a stupid pretence into an experience he made sure I enjoyed.

He didn't have to do that, just like he didn't have to make me feel good about myself.

Yet he had.

'You're wrong,' I said thickly. 'You're worth more than you think you are. And I think you deserve a lot. In fact, I think you might need it.'

He gave a bitter laugh. 'I don't need anything.'

'You do. You need someone who cares about you.'

The look in his eyes glowed briefly. Then the glow faded, his expression hardening. 'It doesn't matter what we need or deserve. I can't care. That's the whole goddamn point.'

I couldn't concentrate. He'd said he couldn't care… Did that mean, on some level, he did?

My insides went into free fall, spinning around and around, full of that ridiculous wild hope I'd felt the day I'd tried on wedding dresses.

I shouldn't have asked, but I couldn't stop myself. 'You…care about me?'

'I'm trying not to.' His beautiful mouth twisted. 'It's a weakness. A vulnerability. And once you've given that to someone they'll exploit it, believe me. That's human nature.' His thumb pressed gently on the centre of my palm, his eyes gleaming. 'I won't be weak, Vita. Remember, I told you. I can't give that power to anyone else ever again.'

My insides stopped spinning, a chill settling in my heart.

So he did care. But he didn't want to and, hell, I could understand that, especially after what he'd gone through at fifteen.

I should have agreed then, let him drive me home, let our affair end. It would have been the dignified, mature way to go. But I wasn't ready and I didn't want it to end, and if there were only a couple of days to go then I wanted them. I wanted each and every damn one.

It might end up breaking me, but that I could deal with later. There were some things that only Leon could give me. Things I didn't want anyone else to give me but him. And I had a feeling that, after all of this was over, there would remain things that I would only ever give to him.

'Thanks for the heads-up,' I said, everything in me aching as the hope I hadn't even realised I'd been nurturing died. 'But, like I already told you, I don't need you to care and I don't want you to anyway.' I swallowed past the lump in my throat. 'You can give me this one thing, though. You promised the "I Love You Girl" her happy ending. And I want it. And that includes hot sex until the wedding day.'

He didn't say anything, and I wondered if he was going to refuse.

I didn't want to beg but I would. For this. For him.

His gaze focused, a laser of molten gold, making my breath catch. 'What can I give you that someone else couldn't?'

I could feel the atmosphere in the car change and I knew that somehow this question was important to him and that my answer was going to matter.

So I gave him the truth. Because he deserved that too.

'You understand me.' I let him see everything in my eyes. 'You know what happened to me and you understand what it did to me, and you wanted to make it better. And you did. You made me feel good about myself and you made me feel strong. I trust you, Leon. No one else can give me that. No one but you.'

He remained quiet a moment longer, his gaze on mine. Then he lifted my hand and pressed a kiss to my palm, his mouth warm. 'Another few days, until the wedding then.' There was a warning in his eyes. 'But that's all, vixen. That's all I can give you.'

'I know,' I answered. 'I'm okay with that.'

And I tried to tell myself I would be.

CHAPTER TWENTY-TWO

Vita

'REMEMBER, YOU DON'T have to do anything but get out of the car, go up the church steps, walk down the aisle and say the vows.' Dad gave me a forced smile. 'Nothing to be nervous about.'

'I'm not nervous, Dad,' I said. 'But thank you.'

Maybe if I kept telling myself that I wouldn't be, though perhaps it was the unexpectedness of Dad being supportive that made me feel like I had a stomach full of butterflies.

Then again, I knew why he was being supportive. It was in his interest that the wedding went ahead considering Leon was going to pay off his debts the moment we were married.

Leon.

My mouth dried and I looked down at my hands, at the simple bouquet of calla lilies he'd chosen for the ceremony.

No, it wasn't Dad making me nervous. It was Leon.

He'd been insatiable the night before, keeping me up virtually the whole night with his magic hands and wicked mouth. As if he couldn't get enough of me.

Yet when I'd woken up that morning I'd found myself alone.

He'd sent me a text a bit later, apologising for his absence—he had some business to tie up before the ceremony so he'd see me at the altar.

The groom not seeing his bride the morning of the wedding was tradition, but somehow I knew it wasn't that keeping him away. Or the business he had to attend to.

He was staying away deliberately.

I couldn't lie to myself any more. Couldn't tell myself it was only about sex now. It was more and had been ever since that night he'd held me in his arms and told me about the men who'd tortured him.

About the father who'd abandoned him.

He was damaged and, like the cliché I was, I wanted to help him. Heal him the way he'd healed me. But he wouldn't let me.

My heart ached like someone had kicked it.

A commotion came from outside the car and I looked up. There'd been some paparazzi waiting outside the church as we drew up and a couple of them had got into an argument. Were they still at it?

But there weren't any paparazzi there now—the church steps were empty—and the commotion turned out to be my father exclaiming as the limo door was pulled open.

'Get out,' Leon ordered Dad tersely.

I blinked in shock. What was he doing here? Wasn't he supposed to be waiting at the altar?

'Wait a goddamn minute, King,' my father protested. 'What the hell are you—?'

'Out,' Leon interrupted. 'I'm not going to ask again.'

Still protesting, Dad nevertheless did as he was told and, as soon as he'd got out, Leon got in, slamming the door behind him.

Even though I'd only seen him the night before, I still felt starved for the sight of him.

He looked so good—dressed to perfection, his black suit with a bronze tie that echoed my flowers, beautifully tailored, fitting his broad shoulders and chest like a glove. Except his hair looked like he'd raked his fingers through it one too many times and his eyes had gone dark, more brown now than gold.

My hands trembled. I wanted to touch him. But I didn't. I kept a tight hold on my bouquet instead.

'What are you doing here?' Great. At least my voice was level. 'Aren't you supposed to be inside?'

His expression remained hard and something dropped away inside me.

'You're…not going through with it, are you?'

His continued silence gave me his answer.

I don't know why it felt like he'd sunk a knife into my chest. I hadn't wanted this in the first place. So him not going through with it shouldn't have hurt.

But it did.

I lifted my chin, ignoring the pain. 'I see. So, what? The "I Love You Girl" doesn't get her happy ending after all?'

The look on his face became a mask, his eyes darkening even further. There were dark circles beneath them, like he hadn't slept.

'I've paid your father's debts already, and as to getting those investors on board, my brothers can work that one out. But the proper happy ending for the "I

Love You Girl" is to leave the man who loves her standing at the altar.'

'What?' I stared at him, uncomprehending. 'I don't...'

'It's perfect. Don't you see?' His gaze burned suddenly. 'That prick humiliated you, turned your confession into something that hurt you. But this way you get to turn it back on someone else. Me. And I'm happy to do it, vixen. I'm happy to be your fall guy.'

Something trembled way down deep inside me and I clutched my bouquet tight.

'And then what?' I couldn't mask the shake this time. 'You get to sail off into the sunset?'

'That was always my plan, you know that.' His expression softened. 'It was never real, Vita.'

No, of course it wasn't. And I'd always known it. So why did it hurt so much?

'But why can't it be?' The words came spilling out before I could stop them. 'Maybe not the marriage, but you don't have to leave. You can stay.'

'No.' His mouth hardened, the look on his face shutting down. 'There's nothing to stay here for.'

I shouldn't let him know how much that hurt. I should protect myself, act like I didn't feel the knife he was twisting in my chest.

But I'd never been very good at pretend.

'Not even your brothers? Not even me?' My voice cracked on the last word.

'Vita...'

Impulsively I reached out to put my hand on his, desperate to feel the warmth of his skin, to make a connection. 'Stay, Leon. We don't have to go through with the wedding if you don't want to. But stay. Stay with me.'

His tawny head was bent, the light through the window turning strands of it into gold. Carefully, as though it was made out of porcelain, he took my hand from his and laid it back in my lap.

'It's perfect,' he said, expressionless. 'This way you'll get everything you want.'

Anger and pain tangled in a ball in my chest and, just like that, I was done with hiding. This was important. More important than protecting myself. More important than my fear of being hurt again or of being humiliated and shamed.

He was more important.

'Yes, I'll get everything I want,' I said clearly. 'Everything except you.'

He looked up, his eyes dark. 'Vita, you can't—'

'That might be a happy ending for the "I Love You Girl",' I went on right over the top of him. 'But I'm not the "I Love You Girl" any more, and that's not the happy ending I want for me.' A helpless tear slid down my cheek, ruining my make-up, but I didn't care. I didn't wipe it away. 'Not when my happy ending has you in it.'

Gold flared in his eyes, bright and sharp.

Then it died.

'That's the one thing I can't give you, Vita. And you know why. It's a chemical reaction, that's what you told me and you're right. That's all it is.'

My heart squeezed tight in anguish. I'd thought I was so smart to tell him that, being the scientist and taking emotion out of it, reducing everything to a simple chemical reaction.

But it was so much more than that.

Suddenly I was angry—angrier than I'd ever been

in my entire life. 'And I was wrong. You know what else I know? I know you're letting your past stop you from having what you really want. I know you think you don't deserve it. And I know you didn't listen when I told you that you do, that you deserve everything.' My knuckles were white where they clutched my bouquet and my chest was full of hot stones. 'I know you're nothing but a bloody coward.'

'Vita—'

But I'd had enough.

I leaned forward, looking him in the eye. 'I'm sick of men choosing my story for me. So today I'm choosing for myself. I'm not going home. I'm getting out of this car and I'm walking up that damn aisle. And if you decide not to be there too then that's fine. That's your choice. But if you don't come, you're not the man I thought you were.'

There were tears on my cheeks but I didn't care.

I turned and pushed open the door.

Then I got out and went up the church steps without looking back.

CHAPTER TWENTY-THREE

Leon

I WATCHED VITA walk up the steps to the church in her ivory gown with her hair full of flowers, feeling like she'd gouged a great hole in my chest.

She wasn't wrong. It was all chemicals and soon those would burn out and what would she be left with?

A coward. A weak, useless piece of shit.

I was lead, not gold, didn't she know that? Didn't she understand?

A few days earlier, the night I'd taken her so hard on the seat of the limo, I'd been certain that ending our affair would be the right thing to do. She was getting under my guard, becoming a weakness I couldn't afford, a crack in my already badly patched armour.

Then, to make matters worse, she'd told me that she wanted me. That she needed me. Only me, no one else. And I hadn't been able to refuse her. Even though every damn threat sense I had was going haywire, telling me I had to protect myself because she was stealing my control, sapping my power.

Xander had been right that night in the nightclub.

Women were dangerous and Vita Hamilton was the most dangerous one of all.

But no one had needed me before. My brothers all had their own problems and my mother had died long ago. And Dad, well, he'd left me to Thompson, which showed you how much he cared.

So I'd given her those last few days before the wedding, but that was all.

I had nothing else to give her.

You're just protecting yourself.

Yeah, because who else would do it? The only person I could trust to look after myself was me. And if that made me a coward then, fuck, I'd be a coward.

I leaned back against the seat, ignoring the pain, knowing I was right and yet for some reason not feeling it.

I couldn't marry her because I knew myself too well. Once I put that ring on her finger I'd never let her go. And how could I do that when she hadn't wanted to marry me in the first place?

So I'd come up with an alternative, a way to get her everything she wanted. The perfect way for the 'I Love You Girl' to get her happy ending—her jilting me. Wasn't that the best revenge?

Except she hadn't wanted that after all.

'My happy ending has you in it.'

My jaw ached, every muscle in my body pulled tight.

How could that be true? How could a man who'd blackmailed her into marrying him then seduced her, then made her care only to shut her out, ever deserve a woman like her? A man whose own father hadn't thought him worth rescuing from torture?

No, she deserved better than that.

It felt like someone was standing on my chest and I had to open the window to get some goddamn air.

My phone buzzed and I fumbled in my pocket for it, looking down to see what it was. A text from Ajax.

Where the fuck are you?

I hadn't told my brothers that I wouldn't be at the wedding or that I'd be leaving. I hadn't told them anything at all.

'I know you're nothing but a bloody coward.'

She saw me. She saw right the fuck through me. Even from the first moment we'd met, she'd known what I'd always been.

I was a coward. I'd been terrified of the life I'd been born into and my father knew it. That was why he hadn't come for me. Because he'd always hated cowards.

Not bothering to reply to Ajax's text, I reflexively opened the video app to watch yet again the video she'd entrusted to me and that I hadn't deleted, because I was a prick.

The video of her on her knees in front of me, ready to blow me.

I'd watched it obsessively all morning without knowing why, because it wasn't that it got me hard, though it did.

It was because of the way she was looking at me. As if I was the only thing worth looking at in her entire world.

It had been that look in her eyes that had caught me the first time I'd watched her Internet video and it caught me now. And she was still looking at some prick who didn't deserve her.

Except now that prick was me.

'You're not the man I thought you were.'

I wasn't. I never had been.

But you could be.

The thought hit me like a bullet to the chest, an explosion of force and then a shattering pain. I couldn't be that man. Could I?

Depends on how much she matters to you, doesn't it?

I felt like I was balanced on the edge of a cliff and any movement would send me over into a chasm.

What kind of man did she think I was? She'd told me once that my father should have come for me, should have protected me and I'd ignored that. Then she'd said that I deserved to have what I wanted and I'd discounted that.

I hadn't listened to her. I hadn't believed her.

But she believed. She was inside that church, in front of all those people, waiting because she believed. Putting herself at risk of public shame and humiliation for the second time in her life. For me.

She was doing that for me.

For some insane reason, despite the betrayals she'd endured in her past, she believed in me.

It was her choice and one she hadn't been forced into. A choice she'd made for the woman she was now, the brave, passionate chemist. A choice for the future.

'I know you're letting your past stop you from having what you really want. I know you think you don't deserve it...'

She was right—I didn't deserve it. But she believed I was something more than my past and who was I to prove her wrong?

How could I let her stand up in front of that crowded church and face all those people alone?

It flooded through me then, through the hole in my armour, bursting that badly patched crack wide open, washing all my careful defences away.

She mattered. She mattered so fucking much it hurt.

No, I didn't deserve her. But I could try, couldn't I?

All I'd wanted was a fresh start. Well, maybe that fresh start was waiting in the church for me all dressed in white.

Maybe my fresh start was Vita.

My heart was beating like a drum, my palms sweaty, every danger sense I had telling me that this was a risk I couldn't afford to take.

I ignored it.

I put my phone away and I got out of the car.

I walked up those steps and into the church.

The whisper of restless people hit me immediately, shifting in their seats and murmuring to each other.

But it wasn't them I looked at. It was Vita, standing at the altar with her head high, clutching her bouquet.

Alone.

As I walked in she saw me and then she went very, very still.

I began to walk down the aisle, a shocked silence following in my wake and by the time I reached the altar you could have heard a pin drop.

Not that I was listening. There was only one person I was aware of.

She stared at me, her dark eyes liquid, stars glittering deep in them. 'You're here,' she whispered hoarsely. 'Why?'

'Why do you think?' I reached for her and pulled her into my arms. 'Because, Vita Hamilton, I love you.'

I kissed her then, in front of the crowd, in front of everyone, and afterwards she whispered into my ear, 'I thought you didn't care.'

'I was wrong,' I whispered back. 'And you were right. I was a coward. I was afraid I couldn't be who you wanted me to be. But I'm here to try, Vita. You believed in me and I want to be the man you believe in.'

She turned her head, brushing my jaw with her mouth. 'You don't need to try, idiot. You already are that man.'

My heart slammed hard against my breastbone and I wanted to be alone with her. No clothes. No defences. Just us. Together.

But we were in front of a whole crowd of people and there was a marriage ceremony to get through.

She pulled back and looked up at me. 'Is it real, Leon?' she asked quietly. 'Or is this all for the "I Love You Girl"?'

I met her gaze and let her see the truth. 'This is real. You can have your happy ending if you want it.'

That crease between her brows appeared. 'But... do you want it?'

I gave her the honesty I should have weeks ago. And it wasn't spurious this time. 'I've never wanted anything more in all my life. You have my heart, vixen. Can I trust you with it?'

Her smile set me on fire. Then she took my hand and turned to the vicar, who was still waiting, and gave me my answer.

'You can marry us now,' she said.

And he did.

EPILOGUE

Leon

I BARELY GOT through the ceremony, let alone the reception, and I only lasted until we cut the cake then I dragged my new wife off to my Darling Point mansion and I didn't let her leave.

Two days later I left the country, taking her with me.

But not for good. We had a last-minute honeymoon to get to in Greece and I didn't want to miss a second.

'Some chemical reaction,' she said, holding my hand as we took off. 'I should have known that theory wouldn't stand up to any scientific testing.'

'There's more to life than chemicals, my little scientist.' I kissed her hand. 'For example, have you joined the mile-high club yet? I'd be happy to help you with your admission.'

Her smile was the private kind, the one that was mine and mine alone.

There was more to life than chemicals. There was love.

There was her.

Vita. It was Latin for life. And that too was appropriate because that was what she was. My beautiful new life.

* * * * *